ASKING FOR A FRIEND

ASKING FOR A FRIEND

Ronnie Riley

Scholastic Press / New York

Library of Congress Cataloging-in-Publication Data available

ISBN 978-1-339-02764-7

10 9 8 7 6 5 4 3 2 1   24 25 26 27 28

Printed in Italy 183

First edition, June 2024

Book design by Stephanie Yang

To all my friends
past, present, and future

To all the nonbinary,
genderqueer, and trans kids
past, present, and future

Dear reader,

I'm here to reassure you about the contents of *Asking for a Friend*.

Eden Jones is a queer, nonbinary kid. They befriend a trans boy, a gender-queer kid, and two queer, cisgender girls. None of the trans characters are ever deadnamed or misgendered—on or off the page. However, this story still deals with transphobia. Eden struggles with a past transphobic event at their old school, and with one of their new friends' past actions.

Sometimes people aren't meant to stay in your life—something Eden learns the hard way. But sometimes people deserve second chances and room to grow if they're trying to be a better person. Eden learns this too.

There are also on-page panic attacks and on-page social anxiety as Eden struggles with panic disorder and Social Anxiety Disorder.

I have lived experience with transphobia, panic attacks, and anxiety disorders.

If any of these words about queer identity are new to you, please reference the resources on page 253.

May you find hope and joy within this story and know that you are never truly alone.

With love,

Ronnie ♡

1

Mom's late.

She's always running from one thing to the other, barely getting anything done in time. But it means I have about fifteen minutes to hang around the school until she gets here, so after the final bell rings, I stand at my locker. Wishing for the millionth time I could be small enough to step inside it until everyone leaves for the day, I try to tune it all out.

"Oh my god, why won't she text me back?" someone cries.

Laughter, squealing, and someone shouting for their friend to "Go long!" as they throw a football down the hall . . . It's too much.

My chest pounds until I can hear my heartbeat in my ears. I close my eyes and try to run through the list of things in the "toolbox" my last therapist gave me. The only thing I can think of is the breathing technique.

Inhale . . . hold . . . exhale . . . hold . . . over and over again until the noise around me is almost completely gone. Relief fills me when I open my eyes to see that most of the hallway is empty now.

I shut my locker, check the time—that was the longest three

minutes of my life—and head down the hall toward Ms. Barnes's classroom. I figure I'll use the extra time to talk to her about my history homework. I poke my head into her room and see that she's with a student already. A white girl with pink-and-purple hair—Ramona Augustus.

Hovering awkwardly near the doorway, I don't know what to do. Should I talk to Ms. Barnes tomorrow or should I wait here?

"I'll be right with you, Eden," Ms. Barnes says when she notices me.

I nod, hugging my binder to my chest, and step back into the hall.

A minute later, Ramona comes stomping out of the room. I open my mouth as if I'm going to say something, but nothing comes out. I catch a glimpse of hair dye on her forehead as she storms down the hallway, and I don't think she even saw me standing there, jaw slightly agape. She turns the corner, out of sight.

"Eden?" Ms. Barnes calls out, and I jerk back.

My homework. Right. I step into her classroom and tentatively say, "I have a few questions . . ."

"Come in," she says, waving me up to her desk. We go over my questions—I had made a list during science class—and then she surprises me by asking, "Did you want to ask these in class?"

"What—what do you mean?" I sputter.

"Well, they're great questions. Very insightful. They might help someone else if you ask them tomorrow in class and—"

Oh. She wants me to *participate*. I'm always getting "encouraging" comments like that on my report cards. I shift on my feet, untucking a piece of my hair from behind my ear. I wish adults understood that talking in class isn't easy for people like me. I shake my head, hoping she'll let it go.

"How about this," she says. "I'd like to see you attempt to ask at least *one* of these questions tomorrow."

"I'll try," I say, knowing already that it'll be almost impossible for me. I barely manage to get my hand in the air when I have to really go to the bathroom. I'd rather hold it until the break, even if it physically hurts. Asking a question that might make me look like I don't understand? No, thank you.

Ms. Barnes narrows her blue eyes at me, and I think she's starting to get that no matter how hard she pushes me, I won't be able to.

I politely excuse myself after shoving my binder into my backpack and rush out of her room as if she'll chase me down until I agree to raise my hand in class. I know she wouldn't, but the image is enough to have me in a near-run to the closest exit.

One look at my phone tells me that Mom won't be here for another five minutes, so once outside, I settle on the bench closest to the drop-off/pick-up area.

"Hey!"

I blink at the sound of the voice and look over to see that the person is, indeed, talking to me. My lips part, but no response comes out.

I guess that's enough for Duke Herrera to keep talking, though.

"Can I sit here too?"

"Um, sure," I manage.

It's weird that he asked to sit down. Normally no one notices me long enough to recognize that I'm here. I've worked on multiple projects with people who ask me what my name is again. It's so embarrassing to reintroduce myself to someone I know. I always wish the world would open up and swallow me whole.

Duke is one of those kids who never acknowledges me. He's from one of the few Filipino families in our very-white, very-cisgender, very-heterosexual school, and he and I worked on a project together last month. He was kind enough to me that I thought maybe we'd become friends, but as soon as we handed our paper in, he went back to ignoring my existence. Normal people would've felt disappointed, but I was numb to the feeling. I'd thought maybe things would be different here. I shouldn't have ever gotten my hopes up.

I'm back to requesting to work alone, and sometimes it's allowed. Ms. Barnes is letting me do the history homework alone, despite most people being in groups of three. I'm grateful . . . even if she wants me to make a fool out of myself by participating tomorrow.

We sit beside each other, not speaking, until Duke asks, "Do you need a ride home? My brother's late, but we could drive you."

"Um," I hesitate. "No, that's okay. My mom's picking me up."

"Okay, cool."

I catch Duke looking at my backpack and shift it so he can't see my buttons. Hopefully he doesn't know what the flags mean. Most people don't. I also hope he didn't catch a glimpse of my pronoun button.

He breathes out slowly, rubbing his hands together. "Getting chilly, huh?"

I glance at him. We're the only ones left hanging around, both waiting for our rides, so he's definitely talking to me.

"Should've worn a sweater," I answer, and I'm not entirely sure where it comes from.

Duke laughs. "You're not wrong. I like yours, though."

I look at him now to see if he's teasing me, but he relaxes back against the bench and gives me an easy-looking smile. Like this interaction isn't taking all his strength.

"Um. Thanks. My mom got it for me."

I squeeze my eyes shut, cringing. *My mom got it for me?* That's a ridiculous thing to say.

"Cool." Duke points to his T-shirt with the logo of the Toronto Raptors on it. "My grandmother got me this shirt."

But I don't know what to say to him, so I echo his reaction. "Cool."

He doesn't seem to mind.

I've played this scenario out many times, talking with Duke

5

casually as if we're friends, but it's so much harder to speak than I thought. I imagined a new school would somehow be easier, a fresh start, but it wasn't.

This school *has to* stick. I am not going to make Mom worry about her socially anxious kid anymore. She uprooted her entire life and started over for me already. Once is enough. This is a fresh start until high school next year.

I close my eyes, the cool air striking my cheeks.

The familiar honk of our old Kia Rio startles me back into reality. Mom sits in the driver's seat with a bright smile.

"Um," I say as I stand up. "Bye."

Duke looks a little surprised but smiles and waves. "See ya."

Mom leans over to open the passenger door while I walk over with my backpack hanging off one shoulder.

"Howdy, kiddo," she says in lieu of a normal greeting.

I roll my eyes. "Hi, Mom."

"Is that one of your friends?" Mom asks, craning around me to look at Duke sitting on the bench.

"Uh," I hesitate. "No."

"Oh," Mom says, looking out the window. Duke catches us looking and waves. "Seems friendly. Who are they?"

"Um," I say, scrambling to think of what I could say. My mind is blank. *Crap.* "Sorry, I don't know why I said no. That's Duke."

"Does he need a ride home?" she asks.

I shake my head. "No, his brother's picking him up."

"Are you sure? It wouldn't be a problem," she says, pausing before putting down the window. Mom calls out to Duke, "Hi, honey, do you want a ride home?"

"Mom!" I hiss quietly.

"No, it's okay, my brother's picking me up!" he calls back.

Mom yells, "We'll just wait here until your brother comes, then!"

"Mom!" I huff. Quietly, so Duke doesn't hear me, I say, "He's fine. He doesn't need us hanging around."

"Thanks, Ms. Jones! He's just pulling in now!" Duke shouts over the wind.

Mom gives him a thumbs-up, looks back to confirm that a truck is there for Duke, and then starts to pull out of the school driveway.

"So embarrassing," I mutter.

"I couldn't just *leave* him. I wouldn't want some other parent to leave you sitting there alone."

I don't bother pointing out that I sit there alone most days she offers to pick me up because she's usually late.

"So that was Duke!"

"Um. Yeah."

"Cute kid," Mom says. "Very polite. Must make him a good friend, then, yes?"

I choke on an awkward cough. "Yeah, he is."

"So, how's my favorite kid today?" Mom asks.

"I'm your only kid," I point out.

"That you're aware of," she jokes. My eyes widen and she laughs softly. "Oh, don't worry. You're my only kid, Eden. So, tell me about your day?"

She seems to be in an awfully good mood, so I can't help but wonder why.

"It was good," I answer, shrugging. "Nothing unusual."

"Oh, c'mon, I want to know more than that!" Mom protests. "You know the deal."

I swallow, but a lump grows in my throat. When I begged her to switch schools and said a fresh start was all I needed, Mom said, *"Let's make a deal: If things aren't working out, you don't wait until they blow up to tell me. I want you to be honest about how you're doing every day, okay? Even if it's hard."*

I agreed, but then again, I would have agreed to almost anything to get out of my last school. I fidget with the hem of my burgundy sweater, panicking. I search my memory for things to tell her. "It was fine, really. Ramona re-dyed her hair last night on her own, so she still had some hair dye on her forehead. And Tabitha got in trouble with Ms. Barnes for talking in class . . ."

Both things are true.

"And Duke hung out with us at lunch instead of his basketball bros," I continue, my grip tightening on the hem of my sweater. "He told us a really funny story about his older brother—the one who was picking him up today."

"I'm glad I'm not the only one who runs late, and that you had a friend to hang out with," Mom says cheerfully.

"I guess, ha." I look out the window, my mind racing. I'm desperate to switch topics. "How are you? How was work?"

"Oh! I got great news," Mom says, grinning. "Wanna hear?"

"Mhm," I say, partly interested, partly worried. This must be why she seems so happy today.

"I was approved for a weekend off," Mom says, almost giddy now. She wiggles her eyebrows at me when we come to a stop at a red light. "Specifically your birthday next month."

"Oh! That's awesome," I say, smiling, because any time spent with Mom is great.

It's just us against the world, and I can't imagine it any other way. I turn to study her profile now; her porcelain skin glimmers in the afternoon light. Her graying hair is pulled back straight into a tight ponytail as always. It's her usual look for the twenty-four-hour diner where she works.

Not once in my twelve years have I ever seen her dress up. She tells me it's not her thing, but I know it's because our funds are

9

limited. She works hard to pay for everything, especially since my biological father isn't helping with the bills. He was some guy who made pretty promises and broke them all—at least that's what Mom says. Last I heard, he ended up in jail and asked Mom for money. She said no over and over—and I only know this because I heard half the conversation from the top of the stairs while they were on the phone.

She does *everything* for me.

And never takes weekends off.

"I thought tips are better on the weekends," I say, wondering if we can afford a weekend off from the diner. The move to Middleton wasn't cheap—I saw the credit card bills stacked up last week.

"Yes, but it's my kid's thirteenth birthday. I can't miss that," Mom says, reaching out and grabbing my hand. She squeezes it gently. "Besides, I thought I could throw you a birthday party. We can celebrate with your new friends."

I almost choke while inhaling. Pretending that my nose is itchy, I slip my hand out of hers. "Uh, yeah. Okay."

Okay? This isn't okay. This is far from okay.

But what else can I say?

"Yay! Aren't you excited?" Mom asks, grinning widely.

I plaster a smile onto my face, even if everything in me is screaming not to, and nod my head. "Yeah. Yeah, super excited."

Looking out the window, I catch my reflection in the side mirror.

The panic shows on my face, so I attempt to adjust my expression until it's calm and neutral.

Mom squeezes my knee briefly before turning down our street. "You okay, kiddo?"

"I'm fine, but, um, Mom . . . we'll probably just go to Duke's to celebrate. It's our spot, y'know?" I say, and I don't dare look over to see the disappointment on her face. "It's not a big deal, okay? I really, *really* don't want to do anything for my birthday."

"It's your *thirteenth* birthday, Eden," Mom says, and I can hear the frustration in her tone. "We've never really celebrated your birthday with your friends before."

I almost laugh—I've never had *friends* before. A friend, yes. But *friends*, no.

She continues. "I want to have a big party this time."

"Can we afford it?" I ask. I try not to make Mom feel guilty about money things, but I don't know how to get out of this any other way.

"You let me worry about that—but for your information, we can. I've been budgeting."

I wish she hadn't been.

"We'll pick up some treats and a cake from Mama's Bakery on Division Street. Order in some pizza and wings. Your friends can even stay the night—you can hang out in the living room," Mom continues. "Besides, I want to thank the kids for being so welcoming to you. I know you haven't had the easiest time in school, but I can tell this time is different."

"I—"

But there's no way out of this. I can't tell Mom the truth, and I'm not going to win this battle. I can hear the determination and excitement in her voice. There's no way I can break her heart now.

"Okay," I hear myself say. "I'll let them know."

We pull into the driveway of our small house. Mom has to work at the diner tonight, so she drops me off with a quick hug in the front seat. Then I'm dashing into the house, up into my room, to flop onto my bed. I pull a pillow over my face.

Everything's a giant mess.

I don't know what I was thinking. That somehow I'd make it through to high school with this lie? That I could eventually say we drifted apart or something?

I should've seen this coming, but it's happening too soon. We've never made a big deal about birthdays before, so I assumed my thirteenth would be like any other.

How do I begin to tell Mom that while Ramona, Duke, and Tabitha are real people at my school . . . they're not my friends?

That I've been lying about us hanging out for the past month?

That all my stories are made up?

That I don't really have any friends at all?

2

"Does anyone have any questions?"

Nope. None. I know Ms. Barnes is looking directly at me, and I'm pretty sure I'm sweating, but *nope*. I refuse to say anything. I duck my head and will *not* make eye contact. My heart pounds so loudly, I can feel it in my throat. Worried she'll call me out by name, I fidget at my desk.

"Anyone?" Ms. Barnes presses again.

You will not get me to raise my hand, I want to scream at her. Instead, I press my lips together tightly.

"I do!" It's Jackie Marshall, a Black kid with curly blue hair. I don't know Jackie's gender if I'm honest. They wear bright and bold colors, makeup, and rainbow converse. They're outspoken, smart, and sassy, and *always* have something to say about everything. They're intimidating with how comfortable they are with themselves. I wonder what that's like.

Ms. Barnes almost sighs. I can hear it in her tired tone. "No, Jackie, we're not going to get into it now. You can talk to me afterward. But if no one else has any questions . . . then let's get on with class."

I'd be filled with relief if I wasn't so terrified of what I'm going to do about my birthday party. I spent most of the night staring at my ceiling, trying to think of what to do.

Glancing around the room, I consider my options.

Duke is the first person my eyes land on; sitting near the front, scribbling in his notebook. I can't tell if he's taking notes or doodling. He's your typical basketball player, a little tall and lanky, with sort of messy medium-length hair. He'd probably hear me out, but . . . I don't know if he'd help me. I'm a little afraid he might run off and tell his basketball bros about how pathetic I am.

Then there's Tabitha Holt.

She sits a few desks away from me, in the back row, and seems to be folding some paper. Her long, black curly hair goes with the rest of her outfit: round glasses, choker necklace from the nineties, painted nails, band T-shirt, and leggings—all black. She has a round, sun-kissed face with freckles across her nose and cheeks. I chose her to be one of my fake friends for a reason, but I'm not sure I'd be able to crack through her tough exterior without help.

And last, but never the least, I look over at Ramona Augustus. She's probably as pale as I am, with pink-and-purple hair and preppy clothes. Her straight hair is always worn down. She strikes me as brave . . . and commanding. Maybe if I got her to help me, she could convince the others.

The clock moves slowly and quickly simultaneously. Every time I glance at it, it feels like it's getting closer and further from the end of class.

Everything's going to be okay. I can do this . . .

I have to do this.

I don't know what I'm going to do if I can't do this.

I'm desperate, and desperation outweighs my anxiety right now. The bell will ring in a few minutes, and my loose plan will be set into motion.

". . . And don't forget your history assignment is due on Friday!" Ms. Barnes says.

Brrr-ring!

Dang. I wish I had more time.

I'm the first student out of the classroom, so I hover by the doorway. Everyone else walks past me, either chatting with a friend or checking their phone. I swallow, rocking on my heels. I once read that sometimes it only takes a few seconds to perform an act of courage, and talking to Ramona Augustus? That's going to be my act of courage.

It's hard to imagine a world where no one looks up to her. She's brave, tough, loud, and all the things I'm not. She's also one of the most popular girls in our grade because she's on the volleyball team. I can't help but wish I hadn't chosen her to be one of my fake friends, but her name is hard to forget and one I blurted out to Mom when this whole lie started.

Everything is riding on this going well.

When Ramona exits the classroom, I fall in step beside her. *One act of courage coming up.* I barely get her name out of my lips. "Ramona?"

She doesn't acknowledge me, so I can't tell if she heard me or not. This time, I'm louder when I say her name.

"Hmm?" she says, looking up from her phone. She gives me a hard look.

"Could I, um, could I talk to-you-for-a-minute?" I rush out the words.

I'm not sure what I expect her to say—I've run this scenario in my head a thousand times already, each a different outcome. I don't know why I'm surprised when she says, "I'm busy."

I jerk back, freezing in place, and watch her continue down the hall toward her locker, meeting up with Alexandra Jasper and the other volleyball girls. They all start chatting among themselves, laughing loudly.

She's busy? That hadn't been one of the reactions I was mentally preparing for. I shouldn't have said anything. Shouldn't have tried the hardest person first. I barely know how to be around other people, and I hate this. I'm so awkward, and awful, and *bad* at this. Why did I think this would work?

My cheeks are in flames, and my eyes burn with unfallen tears. I spin around, prepared to run to the bathroom, when I see him.

Duke Herrera, of all people, is staring at me with his binder in his hands and his backpack hanging off one shoulder.

Because today couldn't get any worse.

I'm light-headed, and a tingling sensation sweeps up the back of my neck and across my face. I want to run. Run so far no one can ever find me. I never want to talk to another person ever again.

Duke lifts an eyebrow. "So, Eden, wanna tell me why you're trying to talk to *Ramona Augustus*?"

My lips part, but no sound comes out, so I snap them shut. I hate it, and I wish I could react like a normal person—whatever normal is—but I don't respond. Instead, I walk past him as calmly as I can, my hands trembling. I snap them into fists at my side.

"Eden?" Duke asks from somewhere behind me. He sounds confused, and I can't blame him.

Once I'm around the corner, I run. I run with tears flowing down my face. I don't care who else sees me, but I'll be darned if I'm going to let Duke see me cry.

He's too cool for me—something I should've considered when I started the lies. He always has the loudest laugh in the cafeteria, so my attention was naturally drawn to him. He was an easy choice, an easy person to remember. Upon reflection, I should've chosen more low-key people to be my fake friends . . . but it's too late for that now.

I can't catch my breath until I'm in the safety of a bathroom stall. There aren't any gender-neutral bathrooms at Middleton Memorial, so

I usually use the one that gets the least amount of traffic. But that's in the basement, and in my panic, I didn't think to take the stairs.

It doesn't matter, though, because I'm the only one in this bathroom.

Everything is awful. My plan is already ruined, and I'm not even sure where I went wrong. I yank toilet paper off the roll to blow my nose as I lean against the stall door.

I don't know what I was thinking.

One act of courage isn't going to get me anywhere. Clearly I'm not courageous enough. Besides, why would Ramona want to talk to me anyway? She's a Somebody, and I'm a Nobody.

All I wanted to do was introduce myself and say something ridiculous like *"Hi, I'm Eden, they/them. I've been telling my mom lies about you being my new BFF for the past month, and now she wants to meet you. Will you come to my birthday party and pretend to be my friend?"*

Then again, Ramona—and the rest of them—would probably look at me like I have seven heads. And maybe I do, for thinking that this plan would work. I squeeze my eyes shut.

Should I come clean to Mom? Tell her how pathetic her kid is? Really. What kind of person lies to their mother about having friends? Over. And. Over. I don't think a good person does that.

But here I am, in the bathroom, wiping my eyes dry and wondering what I'm going to do now.

3

It takes me a few minutes before I step out of the stall and wash my hands. I check my face in the mirror, and my eyes are red and puffy. There's not much I can do about that now.

I take a deep breath, watching my chest rise and fall in the reflection, and then I decide I'll go join everyone in the cafeteria for lunch. I can slip through the back door to my usual empty table, and then I can get through the rest of this day.

I stop short in the hallway. The bathroom door swings shut and hits my back, making me stumble forward at the impact.

Duke leans against the wall on the other side of the hall, casually looking at his fingernails. He looks up and meets my eyes before pushing himself off the wall. He waits in the middle of the hallway, and after a moment, I collect myself enough to meet him there.

"So," Duke says as if we're continuing a conversation that we'd gotten off track from. "You going to tell me why you were trying to talk to Ramona? Because I think you should stay away from her."

"I'd rather not tell you why," I find myself saying. I turn and head toward my locker because I still need to get my lunch. I don't know what I expect, but it's not for Duke to fall in step beside me.

"C'mon," he says, and my heart pounds faster.

This is just Duke, I remind myself. We've talked for a project before. This shouldn't be as hard as it feels.

Then Duke *nudges* me with his elbow, and I almost jump out of my skin. He tosses his hands up. "Whoa, sorry."

I grimace, but he doesn't seem deterred.

"Tell me, Eden. Did you want to tell her you have a crush on her?" Duke asks, wiggling his eyebrows comically.

If I was anyone else, in any other shoes than my own, I might laugh.

I reach my locker and start attempting my lock combination. My hands tremble with Duke hovering beside me. I swallow before saying "No."

My hands are shaking so much, I have to start my combination again.

"Then what was it? Did you want to work with her on the new history assignment?" Duke asks, sounding a little concerned. He looks at me with such curiosity that I hate it. I'd rather no one pay me this much attention.

"No." Although that could've been a great way of talking to her. I hadn't considered it as a possibility before. I look at Duke after I fail to unlock my lock. I want to tell him to leave me alone, but the truth is . . . I need him. I need him for my birthday party.

"Here. What's your combination?" he asks, nudging me to the side.

I'm so taken aback, I answer him. "Um, seventeen, five, nineteen."

Duke starts spinning the dial on my lock as he continues talking. "If it wasn't because you have a crush or you wanted to work on the project with her . . . then what on Earth could Eden Jones have to say to Ramona?"

The lock unclicks.

I want to wipe the bright smile off his face, but relief floods me, grateful he got it so quickly. I shove my notebook into the back of my locker and reach for my lunch.

"Why do you care, anyway?" I ask, surprising us both when I slam my locker door shut and turn to finally look at him.

"Ramona is . . . well, she's . . ." Duke starts and stops. "It's complicated, okay? And look, I don't know you well—"

At all, I want to say.

"—but I think you should avoid her."

I stare at him, my gaze fixated on his face. He looks a little unsure when he adds, "Okay?"

I don't know what to say to that, so I say nothing. Duke walks beside me again but doesn't speak until we're at the doors of the cafeteria. He puts a hand on my lower arm and stops me.

"I really don't think you should be friends with Ramona."

I scoff; Duke has an easy way of making me forget my anxiety. "You're not in charge of who I'm friends with."

Eden, stop talking. You need Duke. But he doesn't seem fazed. I enter the cafeteria, Duke quickly following me.

"Where were you two?" the supervising teacher asks.

"Bathroom," Duke answers easily. I nod, grateful for his quick thinking.

"Alright, take your seats, and don't be late again."

I leave Duke behind as I walk back to my usual table, grateful to find it still empty. I settle in my seat and jump when Duke sits down beside me.

"Listen," Duke rushes to say. "I'm *sorry.*"

What?

He's sorry?

This makes *no* sense to me. I stare at him, silent as ever.

But he doesn't seem bothered by this in the least. He pulls out his lunch from his backpack and keeps talking as if I've somehow followed any of his thoughts.

"Look, apologies aren't really my thing," Duke tells me, twisting the lid off his water bottle. "But I'm hoping you'll accept my apology. I should have talked to you, even after the project was over. I don't really get your whole not-talking-to-people thing, but I'm thinking we should be friends."

He smiles at me, looking like a hopeful puppy.

I rub the back of my neck. *Why?* I want to ask. The question gets stuck in my throat. I can't ask that. I can't even begin to dare to understand Duke, but I *can* jump on this opportunity and become friends with him. Maybe then I'll muster up the courage to ask him to my birthday party.

Or will he, just like Nikki Gladstone, learn the truth about who I am and mock me? Destroy everything I've worked so hard to gain back?

"C'mon, I'm laying it all out there," Duke tells me, ducking his head to meet my eyes. "What do you say? Friends?"

My mouth is dry, and this is hard. Words are hard. Why doesn't anyone get that? But Duke's staring at me with those big puppy-dog eyes, and I don't want to disappoint him and I need him for my plan, so I hear myself say, "Okay."

The panic starts in my chest and spreads throughout my body. I squeeze my eyes shut and start counting: "Inhale . . . two, three, four, hold . . . two, three, four . . . exhale, two, three, four . . ."

Over and over again.

"You okay?" Duke asks.

I hold up a finger to Duke, practicing my grounding breaths just like my old therapist taught me. I normally do it in my head, because I want to do everything humanly possible to avoid embarrassment, but I can't think right now. Since I've been lying to Mom about doing well and having friends, she doesn't think it's urgent to find me a new therapist.

Everything's okay.

Except . . . is it? Maybe this will have weirded Duke out so much he'll regret his words and leave.

I peek, catching sight of his blue sweater. He's still here—my eyes flash open. *He's still here*, pulling his sandwich out of a plastic bag. My cheeks heat up with embarrassment.

"Why are you still here?" I blurt.

"What? I already told you."

But why? my mind screams. It doesn't add up. It doesn't make sense. Unless . . . "You feel sorry for me."

Duke crinkles his nose. "A little, sure."

Well. That stings.

I bite my bottom lip and play with my hands in my lap, trying to process this. I don't want his pity. And I'm ready to tell him just that when he interrupts my thoughts and asks, "That counting thing you just did—was it to stop panicking?"

The heat rises in my cheeks. The last time I explained this to someone was last year, and it didn't go over very well. "Um. Yeah, it's a grounding technique."

"Oh, for a panic attack?" Duke asks, leaning forward. His expression grows serious. His voice is soft when he says, "My brother gets those. Has my entire life. He does the counting thing too. Panic attacks look like they suuuck."

24

And for the first time in a long time, I laugh. "Yeah, they do."

"Sorry you get them," Duke says. He frowns at his water bottle. "And sorry if I caused it. I've been told that I'm Too Much."

I stare at him until he glances up, and then I duck my head. In a strange way, he's not too much. And I want to tell him that, but I don't know how.

"Maybe we could balance each other out," Duke suggests.

"Heh. Sure." I lean back in my chair, biting my bottom lip harder than usual, and glance around. For a while there, the rest of the cafeteria didn't exist. It was simply Duke and me. And it wasn't as scary as I thought it'd be. In fact, it was kind of nice.

"Why do you want to be my friend?" I ask quietly, finally letting the question out.

Duke looks up at me, almost surprised at the question. I'm not even sure exactly *what* I'm asking from him, but he seems to understand anyway. "It must suck not having friends at a new school."

I meet his eyes now—they're big and golden brown and full of curiosity. I don't feel weird about it, though. He looks at me like I'm a puzzle he's trying to figure out, not like I'm the class weirdo.

"Yeah," I say with a small nod. I look down at the lunch in front of me that I haven't touched. I pick up my apple and nod again. "Yeah, it does."

"Well, now you have one," Duke says. "Can't guarantee you'll like me, though."

I snort. Something tells me that I couldn't get rid of Duke now if I tried. Call it a gut feeling. I realize that he's probably expecting me to say something back. That's usually how conversations work.

"Would you maybe wanna—" I start and then shake my head. It's too soon.

"What?"

"Nothing," I mumble. He'd probably find an invite to my birthday party really weird considering we don't know each other well . . . or at all, really.

He nudges me and nods his head toward the table that he usually sits at with the basketball boys. "Think we could have lunch there tomorrow?"

"What! No." I shake my head faster than ever.

Duke lifts his hands up. "Whoa, sorry. I just thought you'd want to make some more friends or something."

"Um." I swallow. Have I completely ruined this already? I stare down at the apple in my hand. "Not yet."

"Alright, that's cool." Duke leans back and stretches out. His grin is lazy when he says, "But I can't ditch them completely, so I'll have to split my time."

I stare at him.

"What? It's what friends do."

I freeze at the word. *Friends.* Friends . . . *Do* I have a friend? Panic rises in my chest, and I put my hand over my heart to comfort myself. The last time I had a friend, it didn't end well.

"Right." That's all I manage to say.

Duke frowns. "Are you okay?"

"Yeah," I say. I fidget with my apple in my lap some more, and then I add, "I'm not great at this."

"At what? Being a friend?"

I shrug, because it's close enough.

"Don't worry," Duke says with a bright smile. He leans forward and whispers conspiratorially, "I'm the best at being friends."

I can't help but smile back at him. Maybe this won't be so bad.

"So, you gonna tell me why you were trying to talk to Ramona now?" he says.

Annnnd maybe this will be awful.

"I promise I won't tell anyone," he says earnestly, and I believe him.

I shrug, unsure how to respond. I could tell him the truth—I have a feeling he'd get a kick out of it. But maybe he wouldn't. Maybe he'd react like Nikki did when I came out to her.

My mind races with a thousand possibilities, and I finally settle with a lie. "Oh, she knows my cousin. I was going to pass on a message for her."

What?

He nods. "Oh. So you weren't trying to be her friend?"

"No," I say as if that wasn't *exactly* what I was trying to do. I take a small breath and then ask, "But, uh, why shouldn't I be friends with Ramona?"

Duke frowns at his food. "You know . . . a person has to have their secrets, Eden."

I nod. I can accept that. For now, I have Duke in my corner. And that? That's amazing.

I can't believe my luck—and that's the problem. *This* was luck. I have no idea how I'm going to handle Ramona or Tabitha. I don't even know how I can approach Ramona again. She's terrifying. And blunt. And clearly doesn't want to talk to me.

I can't breathe.

Oh my god.

Mom's going to be *so* upset with me. She'll be angry and *worse*: She'll be disappointed. All she wants is a normal kid. One who can make and keep friends. That shouldn't be so dang difficult. But it is.

After Nikki . . . I didn't think having a friend would be possible again. And now I look at Duke, and I just know. I know I'm going to mess this up again. It's going to be all my fault. And Mom will use that tone she reserves for my dad whenever he calls from jail.

"Hey, hey," Duke says, leaning forward. He puts a hand on mine. "Do you need to do that grounding thing?"

I blink at him, confused by the words at first. Then I nod. I close my eyes and start counting. By the time I've calmed down again, Duke has finished his sandwich. "Um. Sorry."

"Don't apologize," Duke says, shaking his head. "I saw you were working yourself up. It's okay, Eden. I'm not going to tell anyone your big secret. In fact, I'm going to help you."

"My secret?" My chest tightens. *He knows?*

"Yeah, the panic attacks," Duke answers.

Oh. Oh. Yeah, I don't exactly want that to get out either.

"Why?" I blurt.

"Because we have more in common than I realized. And I'm starting to like you, Edster." Duke nods his head.

"Edster?" I echo.

"I like giving people nicknames. What do you think?" Duke asks, grinning.

I shake my head. "No to Edster."

"Edie, then?"

"Edie," I repeat, trying to see how it sounds. I've never had a nickname before. I smile. "Yeah. It's okay."

"Cool. So, do you have plans after school?"

I shake my head.

"Then let's hang out. I'll meet you at our bench after the final bell?"

Our bench echoes in my mind.

There's nothing else to do but nod.

4

ME: hey i'm going to hang out with duke tonight

MOM: Sounds good. Don't forget to tell him about your party!

ME: already did!

I close my eyes when I see her text at break. English class was so busy, I didn't have a lot of time to work myself up about hanging out with Duke. I can't believe he asked. I can't believe I agreed. But he sort of makes it hard to say no. He bulldozed his way into my lunch, and I have a feeling that's how he approaches life in general.

I have five minutes until my next class, and all I can think about is how the heck I'm going to keep up the facade of a friendship for *weeks*. Anything could go wrong. Duke could get bored of me. He could learn that I'm nonbinary and ditch me faster than Nikki. He could—

"Hey."

I jump, eyes popping open to see Duke standing in front of me.

"Oh shoot, sorry! I didn't mean to scare you." He leans in, lowering his voice. "Were you doing the breathing thing again?"

"Huh?" I blink, disoriented. I shake my head. "No, um. It's fine. Hi."

"Hi," he says with a wide grin. *Is he about to bail on me already?* "I have to meet with Coach after school, so I'll be a few minutes late. Just wanted to let you know since I don't have your number to text."

"Oh." I swallow. "Sure, okay. That's fine."

"Cool."

"Yo, Duke!" Someone calls from down the hall—it's Trey Danielson, I think. I glance over my shoulder to confirm. He's waving Duke over, and I immediately feel my cheeks redden. This is so embarrassing. Trey's probably wondering why Duke, a popular basketball player, is hanging out with the kid who doesn't talk.

"One sec!" Duke calls back. There's a sparkle in his eyes when they meet mine. I shift on my feet and clutch my backpack to my chest.

"See you after school?"

"Yeah," I say with a small nod. I feel my phone vibrate in my pocket. "Cool. See you then."

He claps a hand on my shoulder like I'm one of his basketball bros and then jogs to catch up with his actual basketball bros.

What. Is. Happening.

I feel like everyone in the hallway is staring at me now—trying to figure out why Duke Herrera has spoken to Eden Jones, if they even remember my name. I shove my backpack into my locker so I can answer my phone.

MOM: Also, guess who picked up your birthday present this morning? THIS GAL

I want to roll my eyes, but my stomach lurches. I grab my binders from my locker before shutting it and heading down the hall.

Someone bumps into my shoulder and my binders fly out of my hands and scatter across the floor.

"Oh!" the person says, startled, jumping back a bit.

"Sorry," I say, mostly out of habit.

"I'm sorry." And that's when I realize I'm talking to Tabitha. I give her a pressed smile before bending down to pick up my binders. I'm surprised when she picks up my journal and hands it back to me.

"Cool outfit," I blurt. When Tabitha glances at me, she lifts an eyebrow. "My friend at my old school was really into the goth look."

"It's more emo," Tabitha says, but she doesn't seem to be upset. She stands up with me. "Sorry for bumping into you."

And then she's walking away as she scrolls on her phone. I hesitate when I notice she dropped something—an origami hummingbird. She's always folding them in class. I smile a little as I pick it up and carefully put it on top of my binders in my arms.

On the first day of school, I saw her with a little girl.

The girl was probably in first or second grade and crying at the edge of the junior playground. I don't know what had happened to her, but Tabitha pulled something out of her backpack and handed it to the girl. It was an origami hummingbird. I don't know what she said, but a moment later that little girl stopped crying.

I guess that's why I chose her to be my fake friend. Someone who seems so tough on the outside but can be so soft and gentle on the inside . . . that's someone I'd like as a friend, I think.

I didn't have time to overthink it, but I do have about ten minutes to squeeze some overthinking in now while I wait for Duke at "our bench." Who says stuff like that? Our bench. We sat here together *once*. But maybe that's all it took? I don't know. Nikki's my only experience of a friend.

"Yo, Edie!" Duke shouts from the school doors when he sees me.

Crap. I thought I had more time to prepare—to think of a reason to back out of this—but he's walking toward me with the biggest smile on his face. Like he's genuinely happy to see me.

I rub the back of my neck and wait until he's close enough that I can say a quiet, "Hi."

"Hey. I realized that we didn't exactly talk about where we'd hang out. Do you want to go down to the basketball court on Bohan Street? The one at the Middleton Community Center?"

"Actually," I say, perking up at an idea. "I have a place."

"Cool. Lead the way," he says, gesturing for me to start walking.

He immediately launches into a big story about some drama going on between two of his teammates, and it occurs to me that hanging out with Duke isn't *that* hard. In fact, he has so much personality that it makes it easy for me to relax. He's not thinking about me and my reactions, that much is clear.

"And *then!*" he exclaims. "John got in the face of Patrick. They were yelling at each other, and it's like *dudes. Calm yourselves.* We're teammates, you know? Like, why does everything have to be a life-or-death situation? So I got involved."

"Uh-oh," I say, and to my delight, Duke's face lights up. He continues his wild story, clearly dramatizing certain aspects for fun, but I'm hooked on his every word.

I barely even notice the walk as we reach Main Street.

"Anyway, it ended with them being weirdos."

"Hmm?" I say, because I don't need to say much to keep Duke talking.

"Yeah, somehow it got all twisted and they were teasing me about you."

"What? Why?" I squeak.

He jumps a little to adjust his backpack and then says, "Apparently it's weird for me to just befriend you out of the blue."

"Well . . ." I point out, almost in a teasing tone.

"Don't you start too!" he protests, and I try to swallow my

laughter. "I mean, let's be real, I probably scare the crap out of you because I never stop talking."

"Something like that," I joke.

"But!" Duke says, holding up a finger. "I have to say, I'm proud of them."

"Why's that?" I ask, gripping the straps of my backpack.

"Not one of them messed up your pronouns after I corrected them."

I stop short, and Duke takes a few more steps before he notices and turns. My entire world feels tilted. Like this is the moment everything goes wrong. "How—how did you know?"

Panic starts to rise in my chest. What if he reacts like Nikki did? What if—

"Don't look so freaked out. You have a THEY/THEM pin on your backpack, silly." Duke steps forward, hooking his arm in mine, and pulls me forward. "I pay attention!"

"Oh. Well, uh," I stammer, caught off guard. Suddenly I don't know what to say.

The last time I came out as nonbinary, it went horribly awry. A lot of questions and accusations, and, well . . . I hadn't planned on coming out again until high school. At least, not officially.

I almost trip trying to keep pace with Duke.

But he catches me and yanks me upright.

"Hey, it's okay."

We stop on the sidewalk, and I stare at him. How is it okay? I got too comfortable being invisible, and now Duke knows and . . .

"I'm trans." Duke interrupts my thoughts as if I'm not having the most horrific flashbacks to Nikki scoffing at me. Telling me that being nonbinary isn't real. *It is.* It is because when I saw the definition of the word, my world started to feel right. I know it's real.

And then I realize what Duke said.

"Wait, you're trans?" I blurt. It's rude, but Duke doesn't seem annoyed.

"You didn't know, did you?" Duke grins. "Awesome! Because before you moved here, I started puberty blockers. It felt right for me—to eventually transition. So I've been on these puberty blockers for almost three years now, and it's been amazing. It's really allowed me to explore my gender without having to freak out about my body changing too much."

I take a moment to process this, and Duke doesn't seem to mind waiting. He's *trans.* My heart starts beating faster. He used my pronouns. In fact, he corrected his friends, and *they* used my pronouns. I feel lighter somehow. Like I can show Duke exactly who I am, and he'll understand it.

"I—I had no idea," I finally say. But a smile flashes across my face. "Wow, I'm so relieved."

"Yeah?" Duke asks.

I nod eagerly. "Yeah. I'm so happy for you. And . . . just . . . thanks."

"Okay, well, I'll be fully honest now, I guess." Duke lets out a little laugh and runs his hand through his hair. "When I saw your THEY/THEM pin, I knew I *really* messed up not being your friend after we worked on that project together. I could use a queer friend, y'know? It's a little lonely sometimes."

"Yeah," I say, smiling at Duke. "It is."

"Sorry I didn't tell you that sooner."

I shrug. "Thanks for telling me at all."

"Sure thing. You know, my parents are supportive, but they don't, like, *get* it. We don't really talk about it . . . so it's nice to know I can talk with someone who will get all the gender stuff."

"Like gender dysphoria!" I say, grinning, a little relieved the tough part of the conversation is over. "Wow, that's not something I thought I'd ever be happy talking about. But do you ever feel like your body is just . . . not showing you the way you want the world to see you?"

"Yes!" Duke nudges me. "This is so cool. I'm so glad we're friends now, Edie."

We come to a stop in front of Uncle Moe's Bookstore, the only other place that feels like home in Middleton.

"Wait, we're going to a bookstore? Could you be nerdier?" Duke asks. My eyes widen.

"Dude—are you okay with *dude*?" he interrupts himself. I nod. I've never been called *dude* before in my life, but I think it's fine coming from Duke. He continues, "Cool. Dude, I'm just teasing you. It's what friends do."

He makes a silly face, and I laugh for the second time today. The sound bubbles out of me, catching me by surprise, but I don't feel as stressed as I usually do when I'm around other people. Something about Duke just . . . puts me at ease.

Besides, knowing he's *trans*? That's a whole other story. It makes everything different between us. He's not going to ditch me just because I'm nonbinary. He's not going to be like Nikki . . . at least, not in that sense.

My shoulders loosen as tension ebbs.

Duke motions to the Uncle Moe's Bookstore sign. "Nerd alert."

"I love this place, okay?" I defend.

"Okay," he says, and it *feels* okay.

"So. I'm nonbinary, you're trans . . ." I start, but I'm not entirely sure where I'm planning on going with the rest of the sentence. I trail off.

"Yes and yes," Duke says easily.

We look at each other for a moment, and I take a deep breath and say, "I'm also asexual. And biromantic."

"Bi, bi, bi," Duke says in a singsong tone. "Me too! I'm bisexual—biromantic, I mean."

Then we high-five. Me! I high-fived someone. Not just someone, but a *friend*. I grin at him and quietly say, "You know, you're something else, Duke."

"I know, I know. I'm Too Much sometimes."

"Maybe, but not for me." I nudge him with my elbow. "Shall we go inside?"

"You lead, I'll follow," he says, grinning.

5

When we enter Uncle Moe's, I immediately head for the cash register to say hi to Uncle Moe. I don't even think about it anymore. I spent most of my summer here, and the first month of school. It's become my haven.

When Uncle Moe sees me, he beams. "Eden! How is my favorite customer today?"

"Good," I answer, grinning. I feel light today. Lighter than I have in *ages*. Duke comes up behind me and looks between us. I can't imagine what he must think of me now. Was Duke *really* joking about calling me a nerd? But I forge ahead. "Uncle Moe, this is Duke. Duke, this is Uncle Moe."

"You're already introducing me to the family?" Duke jokes, holding a hand out to Uncle Moe.

"No, uh, he's not my *real* uncle," I explain. "He's *everyone's* uncle."

Duke flashes his easy grin and says, "Gotcha. Nice to meet you, Uncle Moe."

Uncle Moe laughs, almost a full belly laugh. Sometimes, he reminds me of Black Santa. His beard just needs to be longer. "Nice to meet you too, kid. Any friend of Eden's is a friend of mine."

Uncle Moe emphasizes the word *friend* and I can't help but roll my eyes. He's probably one of the few adults in my life who truly knows me other than Mom. It's easier to talk to adults than kids my own age sometimes.

"This place smells good," Duke comments, looking around.

"That's because Uncle Moe added a bakery counter to it last summer," I tell Duke. I feel more confident talking to him on my turf. "He's got the best chocolate brownies you'll ever have."

"Ooh," Duke says, eyes sparkling. "I'll have to try some."

"Go on," Uncle Moe says to Duke. "Tell Kevin it's on the house, courtesy of Uncle Moe. The password is Eden Jones."

"You're the password?" Duke asks, looking impressed.

"I'm, um, something of a regular," I say, feeling my face heat up. Duke just laughs and runs over to the bakery counter. I turn back to Uncle Moe and say, "Thanks. I appreciate it."

"Anytime, kid," he says, nodding. Quieter now, he adds, "It's nice to see you've made a friend."

I glance over my shoulder to see Duke standing on his tiptoes to see all the things in the display. I feel my face soften. "I think he's a good one."

"So do I." Uncle Moe winks at me.

I grin, because Uncle Moe's stamp of approval means the world.

"Oh, what about your chocolate banana bread?" I hear Duke ask Kevin.

"I should get him before he eats everything you have," I find myself saying. Uncle Moe gives me a wink. I'm surprised at how easily Duke fits into my little world here.

"What are you doing?"

"Trying a little bit of everything," Duke answers. "It all looks so good."

I laugh for another time today. "What are you getting?"

"The brownies for us since they're on the house, and I'm buying some chocolate fudge for my brother—it's his favorite—and chocolate banana bread. And a muffin. But that's for breakfast tomorrow."

I shake my head in disbelief and give Kevin a shy smile.

"Alright," Duke says once he's gotten his order. "Show me around."

"Oh, I thought we could just sit at the back—"

"And miss a grand tour of your favorite place?" Duke asks. "No way, Edie."

I groan a little but nod in agreement. Uncle Moe's Bookstore has three levels, but my favorite is the first. It has everything I could possibly need. The second and third levels are more for adults and stuffy topics.

"Ah, the sweet sound of reluctant acceptance," Duke teases. "It'll be okay."

"Ugh," I say, and this time I see a flicker of hesitation in Duke's eyes—like he's not sure how to read me. I say the only thing I can think of: "You're the worst."

It works. A smile is back on his face, and he puffs his chest. Duke bumps my elbow with his. "Alright, lead on."

I suddenly feel shy, sharing this part of me with him. But I remember that he's trans, so he gets me on levels that Mom doesn't even get. And *that* counts for a lot.

We walk around the first level.

Bringing Duke into my favorite place was A Choice. He darts through the shelves looking for the middle-grade books to peruse. When I meet up with him, he has his hands on this awesome series I recently read. I bend down to get on Duke's level.

"That series is great."

"Yeah? I've been meaning to read them but . . ."

"You can borrow my copies, if you want," I offer.

"Sweet, I'd love that." He puts the book back onto the shelf. "So, you read a lot, right?"

"Yep." I stand up, browsing the shelves. "Oh! If you want a good read, there's this book. The main character is a trans boy. Basically he joins a hockey team and it's about his journey for getting acceptance from his teammates. It's good. I don't own it, but I borrowed it from the library."

"Cool," Duke says, but he gives me a funny look.

"What?" I ask.

"You're not as quiet as I thought." Duke smiles at me. "It's nice. Surprising, but nice."

I rub the back of my neck, unsure how to respond to that.

"Don't look so worried. I like you, Edie. You're pretty cool to hang with," Duke says, almost beaming.

My hands tremble as I cover my mouth with them. I feel a little shaky, but then I manage to whisper, "No one's ever said anything like that to me before."

Duke wraps an arm around my shoulders. His eyes squint at me, lit with an inner glow, and then he says, "Stick with me, Eden Jones. I've got you."

I smile at him.

I bring Duke to the little reading nooks that Uncle Moe crafted by hand and the section of tables at the back, where we finally sit at my usual spot. It's strange having someone sitting across from me.

"I get why you love this place," Duke says, nodding with approval. He smiles and takes a bite out of his chocolate brownie. "Mmm. Almost as good as Mama's Bakery."

"I've only had their cheesecakes," I admit.

"To be fair, their cheesecakes are legendary," Duke says, nodding in agreement. "Mmm. Okay, but this chocolate banana bread is out of this world."

I laugh—for a fourth time? Fifth? I might have lost count already—and grab a piece off the slice that Duke holds out. We sit in silence for a moment, just enjoying the baked goods. And I can't help but feel hopeful.

I catch Uncle Moe's watchful gaze a while later when he's restocking the shelves. He gives me a wink, and I settle back into my chair.

Maybe things are looking up after all.

"I should go," Duke says, looking at the time. "My mom expects me home soon. But I'll catch up with you tomorrow?"

"Sure."

"Let's trade numbers before I go," Duke suggests, holding out his phone to me. I blink and put my number into his phone. This is the first time I've ever done something like this.

"Now that you have my number, will you text me when you get home?" I ask, and when Duke rolls his eyes, I stick out my tongue. "Humor me."

"Okay, okay. I'll text you when I get home. You're such a worrywart. See you."

I pull out my homework. I start working, but my mind keeps dashing to the current problem at hand: How do I get Tabitha to be my friend? And worse, how is Duke going to feel when I try to talk to Ramona again?

It feels like I've finally found my footing with someone my age . . . I'm not sure I'm ready to lose that so soon.

I close my eyes and internally groan.

"Hey, Eden," I hear Kevin say.

I open my eyes to see him standing in front of me. It takes me a moment, but I manage to say "Hey."

"I found a book you might like," Kevin tells me. He hands it over to me.

I'd protest that I don't solely read queer books, but then I think of the last books I've read. I reach out to take it from him. I read the back of it, smiling as I realize it's about a nonbinary kid, and when I look up to say thanks to Kevin, he's gone. He might be more awkward than me. And that's saying something.

But an idea strikes me—what if . . . What if I meet Tabitha on her turf? She might be more comfortable befriending me. Just like I'm more comfortable around Duke when we're at Uncle Moe's Bookstore versus at school.

A plan starts formulating.

6

I decided to swing by my mom's diner for dinner tonight. I could've had a sandwich at Uncle Moe's, but I used up most of my allowance and I'm not about to break into my piggy bank for some food even if I get a discounted meal.

"Eden!" Mom says cheerfully when she spots me. She's clearing a table, but she sets down her tray and gives me a hug. "I think one of your friends is here, actually."

"Wh-what?" I stammer. *Can't I catch a break?*

"I want to say it's Tabitha. I mean, I only saw the few Instagram photos you showed me, so I can't be too sure," Mom says. She continues to clear the table but nods to the corner. "Over there, with some of the other people from the Middleton Community Center."

I look over, freezing when I spot Tabitha Holt sitting there with some older people.

"Isn't that her?"

"Uhhh," I start, but I'm not sure what to say.

"You should go say hi," Mom says. "Maybe she'll keep you company tonight."

"I don't—I don't want to bother her," I say.

"Go say hi!" Mom encourages. "I'll bring her over a milkshake, on the house."

Before I can tell Mom not to, she's walking to the back counter. Everything is about to blow up if I don't do damage control. I rush over to Tabitha's table and stand awkwardly there until she notices me.

"Hi?" Tabitha says.

Her community center friends stare at me too.

I did not think this through. I'm about to spin on my heel and get as far away from her as I can when I hear the milkshake machine whirling. *Crap.* "Um, hi. Just wanted to say thank you for helping me with, uh, my binders and stuff."

"Okaaaay," Tabitha says, drawing out the word. The adult beside her nudges her with their elbow. "No problem."

Mom comes up at that exact moment and sets down the milkshake. "Well, hello, Tabitha! I'm Eden's mom. They've told me so much about you."

". . . okay," Tabitha says after a moment. She glances at me, a quizzical expression on her face.

"Mostly about your cool outfits," I blurt, hoping that's not creepy.

Mom laughs. "Yes, a lot about your cool outfits. But I've seen you here before; I'm sorry for never introducing myself. I've got a milk-shake coming for you—it's on the house, of course."

I need her to stop talking now.

"Great, you've met! Anyway, I just wanted to say hi. See you at school." A large group of high schoolers come barreling into the diner. "Mom! You have some customers!"

I turn on my heel, grab my mom's arm, and steer her back to my usual booth on the other side of the diner. "She's in the middle of an important meeting; we don't need to bother her."

"Oh!" Mom glances back and then says, "I didn't realize. Why don't you take a seat?"

"Thanks," I say.

Mom goes to greet the high schoolers.

And just like that, I take my seat in the booth with my back to Tabitha and slump down. *Whew.* How on earth am I supposed to keep this up? I'm just grateful they didn't sit in Mom's section, so Mom didn't introduce herself before I got here.

I eat quickly, thank Mom, and get my stuff together. Mom swings by again and says, "You should say goodbye to Tabitha before you head out."

"We were texting," I lie again. "She's busy with her community center people. It's okay, Mom. Honestly."

"Okay. You know best," Mom says. She wraps me up in

another hug. "Text me when you get home?"

"Okay," I say. "Love you."

"Love you too."

And then I get the heck out of there.

7

ME: i'm hanging out with Duke today after school!

MOM: Have fun!

ME: i can't hang out tonight—mom just texted and i have to do some chores around the house. sorry, duke! 🙁

DUKE: no worries! 😊

I wince as I slip my phone into my pocket. Lying to both Mom and Duke doesn't feel great, but I can't risk either finding out the truth.

As soon as the bell rings for the end of the day, I dart down the hall and shove my binders into my backpack. I slam my locker door shut with a little more force than usual and duck past Duke and his friends.

I turn down the hall and that's when I see her: Tabitha Holt.

She walks down the hallway, talking to someone on the phone.

"I don't know why they'd say that," I overhear her say. "I've been doing my best."

I try to be as casual as possible because I don't want to spook her. I'm going to do some recon on Tabitha today, see her on her own turf, and gather information that might make it easier to befriend her. I have no plans on actually talking to her, just scribbling down some notes in my journal.

"Well, that's obviously not true," Tabitha snaps to whoever is on the phone.

Why did I tell Mom I'm friends with her? I have no idea. We obviously have nothing in common.

But I follow her out of the school, not close enough to hear any more of her conversation, and down the street. Is she planning on going to the community center? I only know she likes to do art there because our art teacher used her as an example to encourage the rest of us to go.

I only duck behind a tree once, but otherwise, I end up following Tabitha to the community center, my heart in my throat the entire time. She slips inside and I stay back on the sidewalk. Now what?

"Eden?"

I freeze. *Crap.* That's definitely Duke's voice.

Turning on my heel, I plaster an awkward smile on my face. Duke tosses a basketball to Trey before jogging over.

"Hey," he says when he gets to me. "Everything okay?"

"Huh?" I blurt.

"Well, first you bail on me. Now you're here?" Duke asks. "So, is everything okay?"

Oh my god. He doesn't know I lied to him. He thinks I came look-ing for him. I square my shoulders slightly and nod. "Yeah, um, turns out Mom doesn't need me to do any chores right after school. She's, uh, got a night shift so I can, um, do them later."

Duke's smile makes my stomach ache. "Cool. I promised the guys I'd play with them for a bit, but you're welcome to watch us."

"Sounds good." I pause, an idea flashing in my head. "I'm just going to use the community center's bathroom first."

Duke nods. "Okay. I'll see you down at the courts?"

"Sure."

"Awesome!"

I rush inside the community center.

How could I have thought of everything *except* that if I bailed, Duke would likely play basketball at the community court beside the center?

I'm ready to pull the plug on my idea and just go watch him play when I bump into someone turning the corner.

"Oof!"

I stumble back, freezing when I realize that I've just run into Tabitha, *literally* for the second time, and made her spill all her col-ored pencils everywhere. "Oh! I'm sorry!"

Immediately I scramble to pick some up.

"It's fine," Tabitha says, but it doesn't *sound* fine. She collects a bunch of them quicker than I do, and sighs when she holds her hand out.

I place the ones that I picked up in her hand and she tucks them back into the jar she had been carrying them in.

"Sorry, um. We should stop meeting like this?" I try to joke, but my words are strangled, and I swallow hard.

Tabitha doesn't crack a smile. Instead, she asks, "What are you doing here?"

"Sorry. I, uh, I was looking for the bathroom?" I find myself asking. *Why?* That's so embarrassing—I shouldn't have said anything and—

"They're down the hall," Tabitha says, pointing in the opposite direction of where I was walking. "Take the first left."

"Oh." My face flushes with heat. "Um. Thank you."

"Sure." Tabitha pauses before saying, "Eden Jones, right?"

She knows my name?

"Uh, yeah," I manage. She gives me an odd look. I run a hand through my short hair and let out a deep breath. "Tabitha Holt?"

She nods. "Yeah. So, why were you following me today?"

My eyes widen.

"You weren't exactly subtle." Tabitha motions for us to walk down the hall together, but my feet are glued to the ground. *She knew I was following her?*

"Duke!" I blurt.

"What?"

"Duke, uh, Duke Herrera is my friend. Playing basketball." *Ugh*. I can't even form full sentences. How on earth am I supposed to make a friend out of Tabitha when I sound like a mess?

Tabitha presses her lips together, suppressing a smile. She motions again, and this time my legs seem to follow her silent command. We fall in step beside each other and keep a slow pace.

"I see. So it wasn't you who darted behind a tree?"

"You saw that?" I exclaim.

Tabitha laughs fully now, but it doesn't feel like a mocking laugh. She seems more amused than anything. I think. I have no idea. Maybe I'm misreading this and maybe—

"Is this because of Benji?"

"Huh?"

"Benjamin Lasso. Duke's friend. He's obsessed with me?"

I have no idea what to say to that, so I nod my head thoughtfully while my mind races. There's a Benjamin on Duke's basketball team, is that who she means? I don't know if he likes-likes Tabitha—

But before I can finish thinking it through, she sighs.

"I hate it when boys don't understand that no means no," Tabitha says.

Oh, *no*. I didn't mean to nod yes to her question.

She pushes a piece of hair from her face. "But why did he send you?"

"Uh," I start but panic. "He wants you to watch him play!"

Tabitha nods. "Yeah, I was afraid of that."

I try backpedaling. "But just as friends."

She raises an eyebrow. "Really?"

"Yeah," I say, nodding. "He, um, respects your decision, and uh . . . wants you to watch him as a sign of, like, peace?"

"Alright, well, I suppose I can come watch the game with you."

My eyes widen. *What? That worked?*

"You will?"

"Yeah. I mean, we were friends before he decided he liked me," Tabitha says. She comes to a stop and points to the bathroom door. "I'll put my art stuff away and meet you in the lobby in a few?"

"Um. Sure."

I go into the single-stall bathroom and shut the door behind me. I have no idea what just happened. Tabitha's a lot nicer than she comes across, with her black outfits and her choker necklace from the nineties. I stare at my reflection, trying to process it.

She's going to sit with me outside to watch Duke's basketball game. A laugh of disbelief escapes me.

"What?" I whisper to no one. "What just happened?"

Could making friends be so easy? It doesn't guarantee that Tabitha will come to my party, and that's what I need her for. But it does feel like a step in the right direction.

I take another breath, wash my hands, and then go to the lobby to wait awkwardly for Tabitha. I'm half convinced she was trying to get rid of me by the time she comes around the corner with a smile on.

When we're almost at the bleachers, I don't know what to say, and my mind races with possibilities, but nothing feels right. It doesn't matter, though, because Tabitha sits beside me on the bleachers and then pulls out a sketchbook.

"Do you mind if—?" she starts, gesturing to it.

"No, not at all. Go ahead."

"Cool."

And it is. I don't watch her sketch—afraid she'll think it's creepy or feel like it's additional pressure—and focus on the game.

I never thought I would ever be sitting beside Tabitha watching Duke play basketball.

There's only six of the guys playing, so it's easy to keep my focus on Duke. He's probably one of the best players on the basketball team, if not the best. He's so light on his feet that he bounces around other players with ease.

I feel a little uncomfortable sitting here, watching them. But they don't seem to notice me—other than a quick wave from Duke.

When he scores a basket, I clap my hands together out of excitement. I don't even mean to, really, but he looks proud when our eyes meet. I find it hard not to clap again when he scores another basket, even though it means drawing attention to myself.

"What do you think?" Tabitha asks me just after Duke throws a three-pointer that hits the net and bounces off.

I look down to see that she's sketched me. *Really well* too. It's a profile, where I have a sparkle in my eye, and my expression is full of hope and tension. I snatch the sketchbook from her hands without thinking about how rude I'm being and stare down at my face in lines.

"You did this? Just now?" I ask, excitement rushing through me.

Tabitha shrugs. "Yeah. Do you like it?"

"I—I *love* it. No one's ever done something like this before." I can't stop the words from pouring out of me. I gently trace the lines on the paper. "Can I—can I have this?"

"Sure. Consider it a thank-you for the free milkshake."

"Oh! Um, okay," I say, feeling my cheeks heat up. I had hoped she'd forgotten about that.

"It's not my best work, and if I had more time, and maybe a different pencil, but—"

"It's perfect," I murmur. "Thank you."

"Sure. Thanks for having an interesting face." Tabitha leans back, putting her elbows on the other level of the bleachers. "So, why was your mom acting so weird?"

"Oh, haha, she misses being a second mom to my friends at my old school." I can't look at Tabitha when I add, "She assumes everyone from school is a friend, because I used to have a pretty large friend group."

"But she said she'd heard all about me?"

I bite down on my bottom lip, unsure what to say, but manage a distraction.

"I found this from the first time we bumped into each other," I say, carefully pulling the origami hummingbird from my bag.

"Oh! You can keep it if you want," Tabitha says. "I fold, like, a hundred of them."

"Thanks, but, actually . . . I was wondering. Could you teach me how to fold them sometime?"

Tabitha's eyes shine brightly when she says "Sure!"

And just like that, my mom's weirdness is forgotten.

"Do we have time? When does this game end?"

"Now," Duke says, and I startle, looking at him with surprise as he jogs over. "And for the record, my team won. Not that either of you noticed."

I beam with pride. I can't even help it. I was *totally* rooting for Duke, Trey, and Benji. I don't really know the others. "Whoops."

"I'm just teasing," Duke assures me.

"I'll be back," Tabitha says before jogging down the bleachers toward the court.

Duke grabs his water bottle and comes closer to see the sketch-book still in my hands. He raises his eyebrows when he sees the sketch of me. "I didn't know you were friends with Tabitha."

"Ha, I wish," I say before thinking it through.

His expression twists slightly, but I don't understand what he's thinking. Then he says, "I could help you. If you want."

"You could?"

"Sure. I'm great at making friends, don't ya think?"

I almost laugh, but the truth is I'm in awe of Duke's ability to befriend people. Instead, I nod and quietly say, "I'd like that."

"Sweet." He swings around to look for her, and we both see that she's talking with Benji. My face heats up again—poor Benji. I didn't mean to put him in such an awkward position, but it was too diffi-cult to correct Tabitha's assumption. He looks happy, though.

Duke glances between us, grinning like he knows a secret I don't. He calls over to Tabitha, "Yo, Tabs, Eden and I are going to hang out now. Wanna join?"

I blink. Either they're already friends or he's just really comfort-able with everyone he meets.

Tabitha looks at us, then Benji, and then back to us. She nods. "Okay! Just one sec."

She says something quietly to Benji before skipping over. She gives us a thumbs-up. "Perfect timing, guys."

"Oh, uh," Duke says, giving me a slightly panicked look. I shrug and he nods, understanding.

"What? Did I say something wrong?" Tabitha asks.

Duke looks at me, almost as if he's trying to read me so he can answer. But I find myself trusting him, trusting Tabitha, and say, "It's because I'm nonbinary. So . . . not a guy."

We wait in silence for a split second—but the second feels like twelve thousand too many. Then Tabitha says, "Oh! I'm sorry. What are your pronouns?"

"They/them," I answer. "And it's fine; I don't mind. I think Duke wasn't sure how I'd feel about being called a guy."

"Yeah," Duke says, shrugging. "Just wanted to make sure you were, like, okay with it."

Tabitha smiles. "Sorry. I'm still fairly new to the queer world, if I'm honest."

"No worries," I say. When she scrunches her nose up, I add, "Seriously. Totally fine. We live in a small town in the middle of nowhere."

"No excuse," Tabitha says, shaking her head. She hesitates before asking, "Still want to hang out together?"

"Yes," Duke answers for the both of us. I smile, grateful. "We were probably going to go to this bookstore Edie likes. It's pretty chill. *And* I want to see if they've gotten their milkshake machine yet. Kevin— he's a baker there—said they ordered one."

I blink. *I* didn't even know that.

Oh no, does this mean Tabitha's going to remember my mom's weirdness the other night again? I thought I was in the clear from the Milkshake Incident. I don't dare look at Tabitha when I ask, "Kevin's a baker?"

"Yeah. Well, sort of. He assists the baker," Duke explains, picking up his backpack and hooking his thumbs around the straps. I climb down from the bleachers and hand Tabitha back her sketchbook. She smiles and carefully rips out the sketch of me. I take the paper and gently roll it up so I can carry it with me.

"I didn't realize," I tell Duke as the three of us walk away.

"Bye!" Trey calls out from the other side of the court.

Duke smiles broadly, a smile I haven't seen before. He lifts his hand up and gives Trey a small wave. "See you tomorrow, man!"

Then he focuses his attention back on us and says, "Oh, yeah. Abigail is the baker. She refused to give me the secret recipe for her oatmeal chocolate chip cookies. They're *so* good."

"Mmm, my favorite kind of cookie!" Tabitha exclaims.

"Mine too!" Duke says.

They chat easily about their favorite cookies, and I feel awkward. I want to say something, but I'm not sure what. I blurt, "My friends at my old school and I used to bake cookies together all the time."

Duke gives me a strange look before nodding.

Why, oh why did I just lie again?

"Even your goth friend?" Tabitha asks.

I almost choke on air but manage to get out a squeaky, "Yep. He *loved* peanut butter cookies."

They continue chatting for the walk over to Uncle Moe's Bookstore, and even though I'm quiet, I don't really feel excluded much. In fact, I'd almost dare to say that Duke is trying to talk me up to Tabitha.

"Eden is so freaking smart. They know, like, everything," Duke tells her with his bright smile and a twinkle in his eyes.

I'm not sure how to handle the compliment, so I duck my head out of embarrassment.

"*And!*" Duke continues, "They've got a book recommendation for every mood. They read a lot."

Great. Now I sound a bit like a nerd. Although, the way Duke is gushing about me . . . it warms me up inside. I don't know how else to explain it—he's being so kind with his words.

"Ooh, okay. What if I wanted a book that had mermaids, but, like . . ." Tabitha trails off. "Romance?"

"Oh, easy. There's this one called *Against the Waves*. But, um, it's about these two mermaids who fall in love but can't be together because they're from rival pods. It's a *Romeo and Juliet*–inspired story."

I immediately look at Duke for validation, and he gives me the subtlest of nods, like he's silently saying, *you did good*. And then I feel some anxiety leave my chest. I even stand up straighter as I walk.

"Wow! That sounds incredible."

"Yeah, it's really good," I say. "It's probably my favorite queer mermaid book. The sapphic rep is great too. You'll love it."

Tabitha fidgets with her lanyard before she quietly asks, "How did you know?"

"Know what?" Duke asks, curious.

"That I'm a lesbian," Tabitha whispers as we come to a stop at the intersection. She glances around to make sure no one else heard her.

I try to process her words, but before I can, I blurt, "I didn't! Know, that is. I just mostly read marginalized stories, and a lot of them are queer."

Tabitha covers her face with her hands and peeks through her fingers. "Oh. I feel dumb now."

"Don't!" I protest. "Don't feel dumb. I . . . I . . ."

I take a breath.

"I hope you don't feel shame," I say, softly. "You shouldn't."

Tabitha lowers her hands as we cross the street at the signal. "No, it's . . . Well, it's just that no one at school knows. But I thought maybe you could see through me and . . ."

And I'm not sure I could relate more. I don't have to look at Duke for courage when I say, "I know how you feel."

"We won't tell anyone either," Duke adds.

Tabitha's shoulders drop in relief. "Thanks. Um. I mean, I just thought . . . gaydar is, like, maybe real?"

Duke laughs at this, and I smile. He points to the street we're turning down to get to Uncle Moe's and says, "Maybe for some people, but not me."

"Me neither," I jump in to say.

"Oh shoot," Duke says when we reach Uncle Moe's Bookstore. He's looking at his phone. "My parents need me home for something. I'll have to hang out with you another time?"

"What?" The question bursts out of me before I even realize what he's saying . . . what he's *doing*.

He's leaving me alone with Tabitha.

Duke gives me an apologetic expression that I don't buy for a second. He says, "Sorry about that."

"No worries. Eden and I can hang out."

"Duke, um—" But I don't know what to say or do.

He holds his arms out for a hug. It's an awkward, half-hearted hug.

Tabitha gives me a look as if she thinks my friendship with Duke is sweet or something. I swallow hard.

"You two have fun!" Duke calls out as he walks down the road.

I can't believe he just abandoned us. Well, *me*.

What am I going to do now?

65

8

"I've been here before," Tabitha says casually as she holds the door to Uncle Moe's open. I slip in, panic rising in my chest. "It's cozy."

I don't see Uncle Moe at the cash register, so I just lead us to the back. My usual table is taken by a college student studying with their books splayed everywhere, and I freeze.

"Ooh," Tabitha says, pointing over to the window seat in the reading nooks. "Want to sit there?"

"Sure," I manage to say, but my mouth is drier than the desert.

I set my backpack and Tabitha's sketch of me down on the floor and settle into the window seat.

Tabitha looks out the window before quietly saying, "I can't believe I thought that you could tell I was a lesbian."

I'm surprised she brought it up again, and I want to reassure her somehow. The words don't come easily, but when they do, I say, "It's okay."

She turns her head to meet my eyes. "Thanks. So, is it just me or is it weird that Duke just ditched us suddenly?"

I almost laugh. Duke's idea of giving me alone time to befriend

66

Tabitha is ridiculous, but it did get me here, so. "Yeah. He's a bit of a weirdo sometimes."

"Yeah?" Tabitha asks. She smiles, and it softens all the features of her face. "Me too, I guess."

I take a beat before I say, "Um. Tell me about yourself. All I know is that you're an artist and make really cool origami hummingbirds."

I'm not sure what I was expecting, but it's not to see Tabitha relax. It's opposite the reaction I'd have. She leans into the reading nook a little more and then says, "What do you want to know? I'm an open book."

"Anything," I answer. Uncle Moe once told me that people love to talk about themselves, so I'm hoping that's true.

"Well, I . . . um." Tabitha hesitates before she dives in. "I'm in the foster care system. My mom couldn't handle the responsibility of me and my sisters, so she left when I was really young. And my dad? He's in prison, but we're pretty close. He's the only other person who knows I'm a lesbian. I don't talk to my sisters as often, so . . ."

I'm trying to process this when Tabitha adds, "Still want to be my friend?"

"Huh?" I blurt.

"Usually when I tell people that, they feel sorry for me and . . . I don't know. Distance themselves from me." Tabitha shrugs.

"So it's like your test," I say. "To see who stays."

Tabitha blinks. "I guess so."

I sit up straighter and wait until she meets my eyes. This time, I know exactly what I want to say. "Thank you for telling me that. My dad's in prison too."

Her eyes widen. "Really?"

"Yeah." I take another breath before adding, "We're not close, though. He only calls when he wants money from my mom."

Tabitha lets out a soft whistle. "That sucks."

"I guess. He's been in prison for a few years now, so I don't . . . I don't really know him." I press my lips together. I've never told anyone about my dad before. I don't even know if my teachers know the truth about him, or if they just know he's not in the picture. It's been Mom and me against the world for a long time now.

Watching Tabitha's expression, I wonder what she thinks of me. But then she leans forward and whispers something that breaks my heart. "Do you ever wish that he could be a better dad for you?"

My instinct is to shrug, but I stop myself and really take her question in. *Do I?* Just as quiet, I say, "Yeah. Yeah, I wish he could be a better dad."

Tabitha falls back against the wall and nods. "Me too."

We sit in silence for a long time after that. She mostly looks out the window. I have no idea what she thinks about me, but I can't seem to even focus on that for once. Instead, I'm thinking about my dad and how he let us down. How he messed up so badly that he left us before he even really got to know me. How he begs Mom for money to pay back debts and never asks how I am.

I'm not sure how much time passes, but eventually, Tabitha and I are looking at each other again. I find myself aching to break the silence, but I'm not sure how to begin. There's so much I want to say to her, but I don't have the courage.

"Can I ask something?" Tabitha says, and I feel relief rush through my body. I nod. "Since when are you friends with Duke Herrera?"

A smile breaks out on my face without warning. "He sort of just . . . barged into my life recently."

"People are talking about it."

Panic rushes through me. "What are they saying?"

"Just how weird it is."

I laugh now, the sound surprising me. "Oh. Yeah, well, we're friends now, I guess."

My heart pounds in my throat. *What if people find out my plan to get Duke to my birthday party?*

Tabitha narrows her eyes until she decides I'm telling the truth. She shifts in her seat and then fidgets with her hands. "That's good to know. Didn't want to be an awkward third wheel or something."

Wait. Does that mean we will hang out again? I don't know how to ask without sounding desperate.

"What about you?" I ask instead. "Are you friends with Duke?"

"I wouldn't necessarily say that," Tabitha answers. "We've just known each other *forever*. So we're friendly, I guess."

"That makes sense," I answer. I fidget with my hands.

"You know, I'm not as brave as you or Duke."

I scrunch my nose. "I'm not as brave as Duke either."

"You totally are! Look at your backpack. You have a pronoun pin, the progress flag, and that queer little beta fish pin." Tabitha's shoulders slump down. "I just . . . I'm not ready to come out, you know? It's hard. I don't think my foster family would understand if they knew. It's not like any of them are lesbians."

I stare at her. No one's ever called me brave before. And I certainly don't think I'm as brave as Duke. He made a huge decision by going on puberty blockers and coming out as trans to everyone at school. I just have some rainbow pins on my backpack.

But when she puts it like that . . . I can't help but wonder how other people view me. Do they see what Tabitha sees?

"I'm sorry," I say quietly. "That sounds hard."

Tabitha smiles at me, but it doesn't reach her eyes. "Yeah. It is. Thanks."

We fall into another silence—shorter this time, and not as tense—before I find myself saying, "I don't think you need to come out before you're ready."

"I guess."

"No, really." I'm struck with the urgency to let her know. "I probably wasn't going to officially come out until high school. I just have the pins because I like them—and I didn't think anyone noticed them, to be honest. But then Duke noticed them, and he sort of corrected my pronouns to everyone on the basketball team, and so I'm kind of out now. And I know he didn't mean to be insensitive—he was just trying to make sure I wasn't misgendered—but it was kind of scary to realize that people . . . know."

Tabitha blinks hard and then she nods. "I'm sorry, I didn't realize. That sounds scary. Does Duke know how you feel about this?"

"I didn't know until right now," I admit.

"Maybe you should tell him. I think he'd understand." Tabitha pauses and then says, "But you came out to me?"

"Yeah." I shrug. "I guess I did."

"Thanks." Tabitha smiles brightly now. "See, Eden Jones . . . You're brave. I admire that."

I've never seen myself as brave before.

"Want me to teach you how to fold the hummingbird now?"

"Please."

She smiles and pulls out paper from her backpack.

DUKE: so how was your friend date with tabitha? 😊

71

I think back to how the conversation was heavy for the first half of the hangout. She said it was easy to make a hummingbird, but it took me almost five tries before I managed to make one half as nice as hers. Then Tabitha said she had to be back at her house for dinner. She thanked me for the hangout and said she'd see me around. I didn't get her cell phone number—I was too scared for that—but I have a feeling we'll talk again.

ME: good, actually. thx for ditching us! we actually have more in common than I thought

DUKE: good! happy to hear that ☺

ME: [103242.jpg attached] also look at this hummingbird! tabitha taught me

DUKE: whoa you folded that?! cool

DUKE: what's their name?

ME: hubert, haha.

DUKE: hahaha hi Hubert!!

DUKE: I was a little surprised to hear u mention other friends! u hadn't mentioned them before

I stare at the text for a minute or two too long, but then I dive in and type out my response.

ME: I guess we just fell out of touch when I moved here so it's hard for me to talk about

DUKE: gotcha, no worries

DUKE: btw I won't be at school tmrw. going to the grandparents' for the weekend!

ME: okay! thx for telling me

DUKE: try not to miss me too much

ME: ha ha

9

The next weekly history assignment is keeping me up at night, so before school, I quietly discuss it with Ms. Barnes. Not getting the clarity that I need makes me frustrated because I don't want to fail the assignment, but it was too awkward to continue asking questions. Maybe Duke will know the answers.

I'm in my thoughts when I almost bump into Alexandra Jasper, the leader of Ramona's friends. "Oh!"

I drop my journal and scoop it back up as quickly as I can.

"Watch where you're going," she snaps. Her eyes drop down to my journal in my hands and she laughs, a hollow sound. Her voice drips in sarcasm when she says, "Got a lot to write about, huh? With all those friends of yours."

I dart out of her way. Spinning around, I walk toward my locker as Alexandra talks with her volleyball girls. I don't know her, but in the month and a bit I've been at Middleton Memorial, she's come across as a shallow mean girl. I learned quickly to stay out of her way. Things seemed easier that way.

I'm half listening to Alexandra talk while I'm turning my lock, and freeze when I hear her say, "Ramona is *so* annoying. She's always lecturing me. 'Don't say that, Alexandra.' 'Don't do that, Alexandra.' I don't know why she thinks she's one of us."

"I know," one of Alexandra's minions says. I don't remember if she's an Ashley or a Rebecca. "She's always hanging around too."

"*Always!*" Alexandra practically shouts. "Does she not have any other friends? Like, honestly. She's pathetic."

I frown. I'm surprised to hear Alexandra talk so rudely about Ramona, because they've always felt like an impenetrable unit. I wish I was brave enough to stand up to her, but I can't. My feet are stuck on the floor. My words are trapped in my throat.

And then, as if straight out of a movie, Ramona comes around the corner. She waves to her so-called friends, and they greet her with joy.

"There you are!" Alexandra says, throwing an arm around Ramona's shoulders. "You're always so late."

"Sorry, Ms. Barnes wanted to see me for something." Ramona grins. "Are we ready to beat Hurst tonight?"

"Oh yeah!" Alexandra cheers, pumping her fist in the air. "Their volleyball team *sucks*. It'll be an easy win, for sure."

Instantly I'm struck by the reason I had picked Ramona out of everyone to be my fake friend. I was so overwhelmed on the first day of school but quickly understood everyone has a place at Middleton

Memorial. It was clear in the cafeteria, so I had been grateful to snag the only table at the back.

At recess, I stuck close to the doors. I was ready to go back inside as soon as possible—anything to avoid the confusion of a busy hallway—and Ramona's friends came giggling outside. She trailed behind them, stuffing her hands into the pockets of her sweater, and only glanced at me.

Still, I recognized that look. I've seen it on my own face in reflections a million times, *felt* it a billion times. She looked lonely.

Lonely and lost. Kind of like me.

A sigh escapes my lips and regret settles across my chest. I wish I could tell Ramona that her friends aren't really friends.

10

Today, I avoid people at all costs—honestly I can't get the image of Ramona with Alexandra's arm around her shoulders out of my head. How they had been *so* cruel and then put on this fake persona around Ramona.

It reminds me of Nikki . . . And I push that thought out of my head.

I slip into my usual seat in the cafeteria and start to unpack my lunch.

I haven't spoken to Tabitha today, but I know she got in trouble for being late to class, so she has a lunchtime detention. Not that she would've joined me for lunch but . . .

Oddly enough, I feel a little exposed and vulnerable sitting by myself this time. I've never had this issue before.

I'm not sure what it means. I've been anxious my entire life, and it only got worse after Nikki told me I wasn't nonbinary. That I wasn't who I am. Nikki's face flashes in my mind, her mocking laugh echoing in my ears, her snide voice . . . She sounded just like Alexandra did.

And then I'm counting. Between grounding breaths and counting the senses, I find myself okay.

Panic attack avoided.

I hear some shouting from behind me and I casually peek at the commotion. There are two students who are yelling at each other about . . . Well, to be honest, I don't know what. Wrapped up in my own little world, I didn't catch the beginning of the fight. There are flaring nostrils, sweaty kids, and sweeping arm gestures.

And then it happens: Someone throws their sandwich at another person. I don't even recognize the kids who start it—they're a grade or two below me—but I'm not an idiot. I immediately switch seats at my table so I can keep an eye on it.

A huge food fight breaks out. But thankfully my table is away from the others. I duck when a grape flies toward me.

Ack!

And then I see Jackie Marshall, dodging out of the way, holding up a sweater to protect their natural hair, coming toward me.

They swing into the seat beside me and say, "It's a war zone over there."

Teachers are shouting, trying to get everyone back in line. The two of us watch in silence for a few minutes. Then Jackie turns to me and asks, "Did you hear what the fight was about?"

"No," I find myself saying. My heart thuds in my chest. I don't know much about Jackie, except that they give me gender envy. To be that brave, that authentic . . . Part of me wishes I had chosen them as one of my friends. I didn't because I didn't know their name at the time the whole lie with Mom started.

"It was about whether someone won a basketball game or something." Jackie rolls their eyes. "As if it even matters. It's just a game!"

"Yikes," I murmur. We both duck when a clementine comes our way. I hold up my hands. "This is out of control."

"Yeah," Jackie says. "Someone should do something about it."

"*Enough!*" the teacher on duty shouts. Everything comes to a halt. Within minutes, the culprits are sent into the hall for a very loud lecture, and soon enough, the room goes back to its usual buzz of chatter. There's a hint of excitement in the air, though.

Jackie looks at me. "Well, thanks for letting me sit here."

"No problem."

"Jackie. Genderqueer. They/he."

I blink. This is the *third* time someone has come out to me this week, and I'm a little overwhelmed. I don't know what's in the air, but I feel grateful for this gift that Jackie is giving me.

Quietly I introduce myself: "Eden. Nonbinary. They/them."

We both stare at each other for a moment before a smile breaks out over our faces. There's something special about finding queer people in the school—I didn't expect it, nor did I know that there were so many of us. But it feels like we already share a bond that only queer people understand—although I'm sure their experience as a Black person is different than mine as a white person, especially being from such a small, white-centric town.

So when Jackie asks, "Can I finish my lunch here?" it's easy for me to say "Yes."

11

"You're the kid who doesn't talk," Jackie says, peeling an orange from their lunch. "What's that like?"

"Excuse me?" I say, taken aback.

"Being the quiet kid," Jackie says, waving a piece of orange around in the air.

I'm talking to you, aren't I? is what I want to say. The sass surprises me, and I suspect it might be Duke's influence. But instead, I duck my head and look down at my hands. I wring them together.

"I—" I try but stop.

"Hey, it's fine. We don't have to talk." Jackie pops another piece of the orange into their mouth.

Something about the permission to stay quiet sparks me to speak. "Why did you introduce yourself to me that way?"

"You mean, why did I tell you I'm genderqueer?" Jackie asks, eyebrows raised.

I nod.

"I saw you with Duke," Jackie says as if that answers that. I stare at them for a moment, unsure how to respond, when they roll their eyes. "He's trans? And if you're friends with him, you must be a safe person too."

"Oh!" That hadn't occurred to me. I give Jackie a shy smile.

"He's sort of . . . my hero." Jackie ducks their head. I admire their curly blue hair until they lift their chin.

"Oh?" I ask, tilting my head.

"A popular trans guy on the boys' basketball team?" Jackie points out with a half laugh. "I mean, he didn't have it easy. But he also didn't let that stop him. It sort of gave me the courage to . . ."

"Be yourself?" I offer when Jackie doesn't finish.

"Yeah." Then Jackie's eyes widen, and they say, "But I'm not out to my family. Just my friends. Like you."

"I won't tell," I promise. *Friends?!*

"Thanks." Jackie smiles at me, and I feel special. "It's not that I don't want to be out to my family . . . it's just I don't know how they'll take it, y'know? They're already worried enough about me being a Black kid in a very white town."

I frown. "Yeah, I can't imagine that's easy."

"It's not, but it is what it is. This is where my dad's job took us. Although I don't think me being genderqueer will be a surprise to anyone."

"No?"

"I mean, *look at me.*" Jackie gestures to their hair, their unicorn shirt that reads TRAMPLE THE PATRIARCHY, and their rainbow shoes.

I laugh. Then I worry about what to say next. My stomach lurches as I realize I've been casually holding a conversation with Jackie. But I'm unsure how to read Jackie's mood now, and I wonder if maybe they've only been making polite conversation with me.

"Anyway," Jackie says, finishing the last of their orange. "Tell me how you and Duke became friends. It's the talk of the school."

"It is?" I blurt, feeling the panic rise in my chest.

"Nah, not since Shelby dumped Chad and they had that huge argument in the gym." Jackie gives me a wink. Well, sort of; they *attempt* a wink. "So, you and Duke?"

"Uh," I start, and fall short. I don't really know what to say about Duke . . . except that I've somehow managed to make him my friend under a false pretense?

Jackie waits patiently, though, so I know I have to say *something*.

"He saw my backpack," I finally settle with. "Queer pins."

It's close enough to the truth. I shift on my seat, feeling my face heat up. Jackie nods as if this is totally normal.

"So," I say, trying to swallow the lump rising in my throat. "Where's your friend?"

Jackie usually spends lunch with Frank Vernon III, but I look around and don't see him anywhere.

"Frank? He moved away this week." Jackie frowns at their lunch. "It really sucks. He was my only friend."

Be my friend, my mind screams, but the words get stuck in my throat. Mom would be ecstatic if I made another friend— and maybe, this time, I wouldn't have to *lie* about being friends with them. It almost feels like my interactions with Duke and Tabitha are helping me here, because I reach out my hand and say, "Now you have another one."

Jackie laughs but shakes my hand anyway. "Cool."

We don't talk much, mostly just eat in silence, but it doesn't feel awkward. Jackie pulls out their phone and scrolls through, and I worry that maybe I *should* be talking or something. But then they show me a funny meme of a cat and I laugh.

It just feels strange, and I'm not sure what it means when they take my phone to add in their phone number, but I'm standing a little taller when I get to my locker after lunch.

12

Mom's late again, but I'm in a good mood today after school, so I don't mind. I hang out on the bench and text Duke. Usually I'd just catch the bus or walk home but Mom was insistent that she'd be on time.

ME: how's the gparents?

DUKE: it's good! only one fight so far and that was with my bro about who gets the better bed

ME: haha, who won

DUKE: he did, but jokes on him bc he's beside my gparents bedroom and gpa snores

ME: haha

DUKE: so I heard ab the food fight!!! you didn't text me immediately???

ME: haha, it was pretty mild compared to my old school's food fights

DUKE: u used to get into food fights?! edie, u've been holding out on me

ME: lol hardly

DUKE: did u get involved today? throw some carrots at elijah?

ME: I don't even know who that is, haha

ME: but actually no, I was hanging out with jackie marshall . . .

DUKE: WHAT. EDEN. I'm calling u

I'm about to text no, but Duke's name fills my screen. I panic and decline the call.

DUKE:???

ME: sorry, mom's here to pick me up. later?

DUKE: 👍

I wince. I wish I could've been brave enough to just answer the call. After all, it's *Duke.* I'm generally comfortable around him. He's probably the least judgmental person I know, and I think that's mostly because he doesn't even notice the little things.

When Mom pulls up in our old Kia Rio fifteen minutes later, I feel a wave of relief. It wasn't *that* big of a lie. But at this point, it feels like they're all piling on each other, and I'm having trouble keeping them straight.

"Hey!" Mom says, grinning. "How was your day, kiddo?"

I'm buckling my seat belt when I glance at her. She's been working *a lot* of night shifts lately, and I feel like I haven't seen her much. We've been texting, but it's not the same. I really hate going to bed alone at night, but she doesn't usually get home until well past eleven, and by then I'm too tired to stay up.

"It was weird," I admit. "Duke wasn't there, so I was going to have lunch alone, and then this food fight broke out over something dumb, and Jackie came to sit with me."

"Jackie?" Mom asks, raising an eyebrow. "I don't think I've heard that name before. Where were the girls, Ramona and Tabitha, today?"

Right. I told her that we always hang out at lunch together. I can't look at her when I say, "Oh! Ramona was with the volleyball girls and Tabitha had lunch detention for being late to class."

That much is true. The guilt twists in my stomach, but it's not nearly as bad as when I have to come up with a complete lie.

Mom glances at me. "You couldn't sit with Ramona and the volley-ball team? That seems a bit rude—to leave you alone."

"Honestly it was fine!" I rush to say. "Like I said, Jackie joined me."

"That's nice of her."

"They/he," I correct.

Mom glances at me with a brilliant smile. "Nonbinary?"

"They're genderqueer," I explain. "Similar to being nonbinary, but not quite the same. They didn't want to get in trouble with the food fight happening, so they sat with me."

"That's nice! A new friend, then?"

I think of how they put their number into my phone. "I hope so."

"I'm so proud of you, Eden," Mom says. She reaches out and puts her hand on my knee. "You're doing *so* great at Middleton. I'm so glad we made the move; it's great to see you thriving."

"Uh, yeah, thanks." I look out the window, spying my reflection in the side mirror, and cringe. If only she knew that I've been lying this entire time. That these people aren't really friends . . .

I stop myself. Or are they? They still don't know about the birthday party . . . I'm trying to build courage to ask Duke and Tabitha, but it's hard. They could laugh in my face, bored of me already. And how do I convince Ramona to come to my party? And get Duke to get over his dislike of her?

The weight of everything hits me at once.

The last few days, I've been living in a fairy-tale land where it's all going to work out. But it could still explode in my face. There's no guarantee that Duke and Tabitha will want to come to my birthday, and how can I face Ramona again after her *I'm busy* comment when she clearly wasn't?

"So, are your friends excited about the birthday party?" Mom asks. She wiggles her eyebrows at me. "And are *you* excited yet?"

"Um, of course," I manage to say. I'm not sure how it comes across, though. I wonder if I can plant a seed now to cover my butt. "Ramona might not be able to make it."

"Oh no!" Mom says. "Should I try to get a different weekend off?"

"No!" I blurt. Then I close my eyes and look away. I bite down on my bottom lip, mind racing. I didn't think she'd offer to change weekends. I know how short-staffed the diner is, and how Mom must have worked really hard already to convince them to get my birthday weekend off. "No, it's just . . . a possibility. She's going to try really hard not to miss it, though."

"Oh, that's good. It's so nice that you have such kind and caring friends, kid."

Mom pulls into our driveway. She puts the car in park and shuts it off. I'm surprised she doesn't have another night shift tonight, but I'm grateful. It's been a *long* week, and it'll be nice to not feel so stressed.

"Invite Jackie," Mom says, smiling. "To the birthday."

So much for not feeling stressed.

"Oh, but that'd cost more and—"

"No, no, don't you worry about that. You," Mom says as she pushes her door open, "are a kid. My kid. Don't stress about it, okay? Besides, the cost of one more isn't going to make or break us. We could have twenty kids if you want."

The idea of twenty kids horrifies me, and it must show on my face, because Mom laughs as we walk up to the front door of our small house.

"We don't need twenty kids," she assures me.

"Whew," I say, wiping my forehead dramatically. She laughs again, and it's probably my favorite sound. I love when Mom laughs, because usually she's too tired and stressed to do so.

As she unlocks the front door, I add, "Could we even *fit* twenty kids in the living room?"

Mom considers this for a second and shrugs. "I think we could. Why? Have secret friends you'd like to invite?"

Pop. My good mood instantly deflates at the question. I hope she can't tell—I duck my head and fake a laugh. Quickly changing topics as we step inside, I ask, "Hey, can we have a TV marathon tonight?"

"Hmm, sure. I'm thinking of ordering some food in," Mom tells me. "In the mood for anything in particular?"

"Mexican," I say immediately. Firstly it's my favorite, but also, the place closest to us is pretty cheap so I don't feel guilty for getting takeout when normally we can't afford to.

"Mexican it is," Mom says cheerfully.

"I have some homework to do," I tell her. "I'll be upstairs in my room . . . Let me know when the food's here?"

"Sure thing. The usual?"

"Yeah," I say, kicking my shoes off. I jog up the stairs and slip into my room. My safe haven. I close the door behind me and lean against it. *Wow.* What a mess I've gotten myself into.

My phone buzzes and I'm both surprised and relieved to see that Tabitha is following me on Instagram. Maybe things can still turn out okay. Right?

13

"Don't you *dare*," I say to Duke under my breath on Monday. I reach out to grab his arm to stop him, but he's too quick for me.

"Hey, Tabitha?" Duke says with his usual charming grin.

She looks up from the end of the long table where she's surrounded by people she isn't talking to. Her eyes dart between us. ". . . Yeah?"

"I can't have lunch with Edie today," he explains. "Unofficial basketball meeting. But they liked hanging out with you the other day, so . . . ?"

"Sure," Tabitha says, getting up faster than I expected. She picks up her lunch box and water bottle and says, "Where do you usually sit?"

"Um. Over there, at the back," I say, pointing in the general direction.

Duke flashes me a bright smile, and while I wish I could tell him he's the worst, I'm actually a little glad that I'll have company today. "See, I told you."

"Yeah, yeah," I mutter. I smile at Tabitha when she reaches us. "Sorry to make you move."

"No problem."

Duke claps my shoulder with his hand. "You good here?"

"I'm good," I answer, because there's nothing else I can say.

"Good." Duke turns to Tabitha and says, "Make sure they eat their veggies."

Tabitha laughs. "You got it."

Duke wanders over to the table of basketball boys, where they all start yelling to get his attention. And before I know it, I'm walking to the back of the cafeteria with Tabitha.

Only I stop short when I realize my usual table isn't empty.

Tabitha almost runs into me.

Jackie Marshall is sitting at my table.

"Hey!" Jackie waves us over. My legs are walking by themselves. I feel like I'm not in control of my body when I sit down in my usual chair. Tabitha takes the one beside me.

"Hope it's okay that I'm joining you for lunch?" Jackie asks. "With my only friend gone . . . who knows what trouble I'll get into? Might end up in detention with Tabitha again."

"Hey!" Tabitha says with a half-laugh. "I've only had it a few times."

"Either way, I've been told I should hang around kids who are good influences."

"Like me?" I say, feeling lost. I glance at Tabitha, who simply unpacks her lunch. I open my container of chocolate chip cookies and offer her one silently. Tabitha accepts without a word, and then I hold the container out to Jackie.

"Thanks, pal. Yeah. People who don't correct the teacher in every class. But really it's not my fault if they're *wrong*." Jackie shrugs. "Dang, these are *delicious* cookies."

I laugh. The sound bubbles out of me before I can stop it. It's unfamiliar and strange. Tabitha and Jackie both look at each other before looking at me. "Sorry. Just . . . that's a lot to take in. I don't think anyone should want to be like me."

"Why not? You're cool." Jackie turns to Tabitha. "Also, sorry, our friend here hasn't introduced us. I'm Jackie. Genderqueer. They/he."

Tabitha smiles, but I feel the heat rising to my cheeks.

"Sorry!" I say.

"It's okay. I'm Tabitha. Cis. She/her."

"Cool," Jackie says before turning back to me. "Anyway, you're wrong. Anyone would be lucky to be like you."

I blink at Jackie.

"I agree. Besides, you're the first person who made me feel comfortable about . . . my stuff." Tabitha shrugs, looking down. "You didn't make me feel . . . I don't know. *Less than*."

I turn to look at her, jaw slack.

"Oooh. Yes. That's a great quality to have!" Jackie says, nodding as they shove a carrot from my lunch into their mouth. I'd be offended (not really), but I'm too busy trying to process the nice things they just said about me.

I don't know if anyone has been that kind to me before.

Except maybe when Duke called me cool.

"Um. Thanks. I think you're both way too kind."

Jackie and Tabitha do most of the talking after that, but I don't mind. I'm still processing everything. And it didn't go unnoticed that Jackie said *our friend* when introducing themselves to Tabitha.

I glance over at Duke's table, watching him laugh with Trey. As I wonder—once again—what it'd be like to be as at ease with people as Duke is, he catches me staring. He gives me a thumbs-up and a thumbs-down and a quizzical look. I give him the subtlest thumbs-up and watch the grin spread across his face.

A minute later, my phone buzzes.

DUKE: ask them to uncle moe's today after school!!!

ME: no way

DUKE: do it or I will!!!

ME: ugh, fine

"Hey, um," I say, interrupting without realizing. They both look at me. "Would you two maybe want to join Duke and me to hang out after school?"

Hope blooms in my chest when I see their smiles.

14

"Hey!" Duke says, walking up to our bench. I snap my journal shut so fast—I don't want him to know what I've been writing. What if they all find out the truth about turning fake friends into real ones for the party? What would they think of me?

He asks, "You ready for this?"

"No," I admit, and Duke laughs.

He claps his hand on my shoulder. "It's going to be okay."

And I want to believe him. I do.

When Jackie and Tabitha meet us at the bench, we start to walk into town.

Uncle Moe's shock when I come in with *three* friends might be comical to anyone else, but I just plaster a fake smile on my face, wave, and keep walking toward the back. I can't handle any questions from him right now.

"Hey, Uncle Moe!" Duke calls out as we pass by. I want to smack his arm, but I refrain and just walk faster.

I haven't hung out with this many "friends" before. I'm not even sure they're real friends yet, if I'm honest. They toss the word around like it's nothing, but it means everything to me.

I settle down at the same table as always. The three of them chat like they've known one another forever while I fidget with the hem of my shirt.

"You okay?" Duke whispers to me.

Jackie and Tabitha stop talking to look over at me too.

I nod, but no words are coming out.

Duke nudges me with his elbow. "What's going on? You're usually quiet but not *this* quiet."

"Uh . . ." I say, tilting my head. I meet his eyes now, briefly, and wonder if anyone will ever truly understand.

"Do you need us to leave for a minute?" Tabitha offers. She points over her shoulder and says, "Jackie and I can browse some books and—"

"No!" I say, shaking my head. "It's fine. Sorry. Just . . ."

"Not used to hanging out with so many people?" Duke finishes for me.

"No, I've had friends before!" I say, lying. But then I add, "But it makes me nervous with new people."

Duke nods. "How about we play one of Uncle Moe's games or something? Would that help?"

"Maybe?" I manage.

"That's what we do with my family, 'cause my brother has anxiety stuff too." Duke wraps an arm around my shoulders. "Don't worry, we've got you."

"Definitely," Jackie says. "We could play a getting-to-know-you type game?"

"I have one, actually! It's an app called Perception. It asks a bunch of random questions." Tabitha pulls out her phone and swipes a few things away on her notifications screen. "The only rule is you *have* to be open and honest about everything. Okay?"

"Okay," the three of us say in unison. Duke squeezes my shoulder before he settles back in his own space. I let out a small breath of relief but find myself a little disappointed too. It was almost comforting.

"Okay, the first question is . . ." Tabitha pauses for dramatic effect. "What's the first thing you noticed about me?"

"That's easy! Your smile," Jackie says with a firm nod.

"I don't smile."

"Untrue," they protest. "You *do* smile. And are we just answering for you or for everyone?"

"Oh! Everyone, I thought," Tabitha says.

"Cool. So, for Eden, I'd have to say your calming presence. You're so chill," Jackie continues.

Me? Chill? *What?*

"Duke," Jackie continues, "you're so warm and bubbly to everyone you meet. I feel like we're already friends."

"I'd agree with that," I say. Everyone looks at me, and I forge ahead with my thoughts. "You made it really easy for me to hang out with you."

"And you have a really loud laugh," Tabitha says, grinning. "I'd say for Eden, I noticed that you tend to tuck yourself away a lot. It's like, you don't want people coming to talk to you."

"I don't!" I admit.

"What about you, Duke?" Jackie asks, nodding at him. "First thing you noticed about me?"

"Your hair. What?! Can't I be real?" Duke cries when the rest of us groan. "I noticed Jackie's blue hair first." Duke motions toward Jackie's dyed hair. "And their general style."

Jackie strikes a pose. And then another.

"Exactly." Duke gestures to Tabitha. "And you're jumpy."

"I am," Tabitha mumbles. "But I'd argue Eden is jumpy too!"

"Yeah. They are. But I figure you hate loud noises. Eden's just startled when someone acknowledges them." Duke turns to me. "I didn't really notice much about you at first, but . . . I did spot your THEY/THEM pin!"

"Yeah," I say softly. "You did."

"Also!" Duke says, shifting on his seat. "I can't believe you guys think I'm bubbly. I just have ADHD and don't know how to stop talking half the time."

Jackie snorts. "That checks out."

"ADHD . . ." Tabitha murmurs. She looks at Duke, eyes shining bright. "That's a learning disability?"

"No, but it does affect my learning," Duke says. He glances at me before adding, "My doctor said that it's more commonly diagnosed in AMAB people than AFAB people, but she really noticed it in me after I went on puberty blockers."

"AMAB? AFAB?" Tabitha asks, looking around at us.

Duke explains that AMAB means assigned male at birth, and AFAB means assigned female at birth. Hearing someone my age casually mention queer terms makes me delighted. I stare at him, feeling warm inside.

"Got it," Tabitha says when he finishes explaining. "Thanks for telling me."

"Thanks for asking," Duke replies cheerfully.

We all share smiles for a moment. I've read so much about queer stuff—terms, the history, the famous people who made it possible for me to find myself—but I've never spoken to anyone about it in depth before. Not really.

Mom always happily listens to me when I tell her about something new, but I don't know if she truly gets it. Uncle Moe and Kevin know I'm nonbinary and always recommend me queer books, but we never talk about queerness itself.

"This is fun," Jackie says, a bright smile on their face. "What's the next question, Tabs?"

Tabitha swipes on her phone screen and then asks, "Do I seem more like a creative or analytical type? Explain."

"Creative," Jackie says.

"I don't know. I think more analytical," Duke counters.

They both look at me as if I'm going to be the tiebreaker. I glance at the other table, taken by a college student with at least four open textbooks in front of them. That would've been me on any other day. Any other day before Duke. Before my mom's idea for a birthday party. I would've been sitting there, all alone, lost in my own little world.

But it's not that way right now.

Panic starts to bubble from my chest into my throat, but then Duke nudges me and it dispels. I blink a few times before I say, "Um, is Tabitha more creative or analytical? I think I see both."

"Both?" Tabitha asks. She raises an eyebrow. "Alright, Eden. Let's hear it."

"I think you have an analytical side that sums people up as soon as you meet them." I don't know where these words are coming from, but they pour out of me, and I feel joy as I watch Tabitha's lips curl into a smile like I've nailed it. "And you're creative because . . . you do art and make paper hummingbirds."

"I feel called out," Tabitha jokes. Then Jackie and Duke laugh. And it feels surreal. My heart fills with an unknown feeling, and I don't question it. Not right now. "Alright, I vote that Eden is more analytical."

"A hundred p," Duke says, nodding. "You nailed that."

"Do I get a say?" I blurt.

Duke laughs. "No. You're the overthinker of the group. You probably think before you speak."

I debate how to react, and then realize what I'm doing. "Yeah, okay," I admit.

Jackie and Tabitha laugh.

"Anyway, I'm creative. So is Jackie," Duke announces, proudly.

"Aw, shucks. You flatter me," Jackie says, pretending to send heart eyes to Duke. He doesn't take them seriously. "Thanks, Duke."

"Anyway . . . next?" I prompt.

"What do you think my Instagram tells you?" Tabitha says, jumping in.

We spend the next forty minutes diving into everyone's Instagram. Mine's surprisingly the most artsy one, with photos off-center and not a single selfie. Duke's is all about basketball and memes. We laugh at a few of them and let him show off some of his videos. Jackie's has poetry on it, which surprises me, but other than that, it's filled with selfies. Tabitha's is full of snark and has a dark edge to it that I expect from her.

We flip through more questions from the game. I learn that Jackie's the most likely to splurge on new jackets, Duke wanted to be a firefighter as a kid, and Tabitha learned how to fold origami hummingbirds from one of her former foster siblings.

When I mention that art is my worst class, Tabitha throws a napkin at me jokingly.

We share our silly fears, and our real ones.

Duke: "I'm afraid of heights . . . and losing my family."

Tabitha: "Spiders, and, I guess, no one loving me."

Jackie: "Little holes or bumps in things—it makes my skin crawl—and getting in trouble."

And when it's my turn, I fidget with my hands in my lap. How can I tell these people that my biggest fear is trusting them? That making friendships is hard?

Instead, I say: "Birds, and . . . people not liking me."

We sit with the question for a bit, thinking about our fears and how scary it feels to say them out loud. I almost open my mouth to tell them the truth. The reason we're all hanging out.

I don't know what to expect when I look up at Duke, but it isn't to have him wrap his arm around my shoulders and squeeze me in a half hug.

Tears spring to my eyes, but I don't let them fall. Instead, I choke back my emotions.

"Well," Duke says. "I like you."

"Ditto," Jackie adds.

Goose bumps start crawling up my arms, and then Tabitha says, "Well, if everyone's going to say it . . ."

I feel everyone's eyes on me, gauging how I'm going to react, and I think I surprise myself the most when I laugh. The tension evaporates from the air. "Thanks, y'all."

"Can I ask something? Might be a bit personal. But . . . what's the difference between nonbinary and genderqueer?" Tabitha says a little later.

"Really each person can decide the differences for themselves. For me, it feels more specific and right to my relationship with my gender," Jackie says, looking at me. "What about you?"

I swallow and say, "Nonbinary is all-encompassing, so I don't feel pressured to figure out my micro-label. I think they can be used interchangeably, but it's smart to ask just in case."

"Yeah, like, I don't mind being referred to as nonbinary, but it's certainly not what I prefer," Jackie explains.

"This is interesting, because my—as Jackie says—relationship to my gender was feeling wrong and bad and confused about the body I was born into for so long. When I figured out that I was a boy, I was ecstatic. I told my parents, and immediately got on puberty blockers," Duke says, leaning back. "It was . . . It wasn't an easy conversation, that's for sure. They were supportive when the SOGIE Bill was approved in the Philippines, but it's different when it's your own kid, you know?"

"I'm sorry, Duke," I say, putting my hand on his.

"What's the SOGIE Bill?" Tabitha asks, her voice quiet.

"It's an anti-discrimination law." Duke scrunches his nose. "I don't remember what SOGIE stands for . . . Sexual Orientation . . . and Gender . . . something. All I know is that it was approved a few years ago."

"That recent?!" Jackie asks, shocked.

"Yeah."

"So, can I ask how your parents reacted?" I ask, curious.

"They were okay—well, *now* they're okay." Duke offers us a weak smile before he adds, "But it took them—and a lot of people, really—a long time before they accepted it. They went out and bought all these books on gender and what to do if your kid comes out as transgender. And I wanted to scream."

"Why?" Jackie asks.

"Because . . . they shouldn't need *books* to figure out that they can still love and support me. They should've just . . . *known*. You know?" Duke asks. "It really sucked."

"Not to undermine your feelings," I start, choosing my words carefully, "but sometimes, people just need to know they aren't alone in their confusing thoughts. Books . . . can be helpful."

Duke stares at me. "Huh. I guess I didn't really think of it like that. I just wanted them to get it right away."

"My dad did the same thing when I came out," Tabitha says, and I'm surprised she's willing to talk about her father in front of anyone else. I'm proud of her.

"Really?"

"Totally. It freaked him out that I could know before I was even a 'young woman,' but I told him it was just . . . like that. I've never questioned how I felt." Tabitha takes a deep breath, plasters a smile on her face, and says, "Anyway, I've only ever had crushes on girls."

"Now, there's an interesting conversation. Does anyone like anyone?" Jackie asks, wiggling their eyebrows. I snort. "Oh? Eden?"

"Nope. No crushes here. I can barely handle friends, remember?" I gesture around at them.

"True, true. What about you, D?"

Duke hesitates, and it's at that moment we all know. He's got a crush.

"*Promise* this stays between us."

"Promise," we all echo.

Duke swallows. "Okay, well, you know the really tall guy on my basketball team?"

We stare at him. I nudge him. "They're all tall on your team."

"Right. Um, well, it's Trey."

"Trey Danielson?" Tabitha whispers. She scrunches her nose up. "He's so . . . lanky."

"And funny and kind and caring and when I was tripped during the big game last year, he was the first person to check on me." Duke's hands curl around his stomach. "Don't make fun of me. He's cute."

"No one's making fun of you," Jackie says quietly and calmly. They clap a hand on the back of Duke's shoulder. "Thanks for sharing. Now, how on earth do we figure out if Trey is queer?"

"Who knows?" Duke whines. "I'm pretty sure he's straight as straight can be."

"Brutal," Tabitha says sympathetically. "I've been there. I don't like anyone right now, but I used to have a crush on Shelby."

"I've never had a crush on anyone before." Jackie pauses before adding, "Is that weird?"

"Nope," I say. "Asexual, biromantic, here."

"You're ace?" Jackie asks. I nod and they continue, "That's interesting, because I've been looking into aromantic stuff lately. It sort of feels like it might be me."

"Labels can change as you grow," Duke points out.

"Yeah. And just because you identify one way now doesn't mean you'll always identify that way. Things change, people change, and labels are fluid," Tabitha says. "So if you feel aro, then you're probably aro."

"And if I develop a crush later on?"

"You figure it out then. If you want," Duke says, smiling at Jackie. "It's all really up to you."

"Huh. I mean, I knew I was pansexual, but I didn't really think about . . . like, romantic attractions until recently."

The conversation flitters to other, less heavy topics, and I start to relax around them.

15

It's a Thursday afternoon and I'm writing in my journal. I keep thinking back to Ramona and her so-called friends. Does she know? Does she feel the prick of doubt? Or is she as clueless as I was about Nikki?

Fate is funny sometimes because just as I pause my pen on the paper at the thought of Nikki, I catch a glimpse of pink-and-purple hair from the corner of my eyes.

I slam my journal shut when I realize it's Ramona herself. She's at Uncle Moe's, and her hair is unmistakable, even from across the store. She browses some of the displays Kevin set up in the front.

What is she doing here? It's not exactly a store I'd expect her to come into.

I don't know, but . . .

This is my opportunity. This is my *chance*. She's not with her volleyball friends for once. One act of courage . . . That's all I need. Just to try again. She deserves a *real* friend, and I think I can be that for her.

I leave my stuff at the back of the bookstore and walk down the aisle toward the front, toward her. I hover at the edge of the book display she's looking at before I clear my throat. Ramona's eyes meet mine.

"Eden," she says, and I'm shocked she knows my name.

"Hi," I say, my voice cracking slightly. I glance down at the book in her hand and say, "That one's alright. If you're into mysteries."

Ramona looks down for a moment before saying, "Nah, mystery isn't my thing."

"Same!" I blurt. Then I hesitate. "Um, if you're looking for a new book, I . . . I read a lot. I could help . . ."

Ramona searches my face. She doesn't say anything right away, and it makes me nervous. Did I say the wrong thing? Is she going to laugh in my face?

"Sure," she eventually says, putting the book back on the display.

I quietly lead the way down the aisle while she gives me an awkward smile.

I guess it's up to me to fill the silence.

My phone buzzes, but I ignore it.

"What are you looking for?" I ask, hoping she understands that this is an offering of sorts for friendship. I swallow, a lump forming in my throat.

"I don't know." Ramona shrugs. "Is it weird if I was hoping for something a little sad?"

"Nope," I answer. "I read sad stuff all the time. It's comforting."

I don't tell her that I used to read almost exclusively sad stories because I never believed that joy was for me. Not until I read a story about trans joy. Even now, I still read the occasional sad story.

"Do you like . . . mermaids?" I ask, thinking of the story I suggested to Tabitha. It's not particularly sad, but it's emotionally compelling.

"Not really?" Ramona says, frowning. She runs her fingers over the spine of some books on the shelf in front of us. "I'm not one for fantasy."

"What, you don't believe mermaids exist?" I ask, surprising myself. Ramona lifts her face and looks at me, eyes sparkling.

"I didn't say that."

We share a small smile. A moment of silence passes between us before I think of a book. "Do you like poetry?"

"I do," Ramona says, looking at me with curiosity.

"I have the perfect book for you, then," I say, scanning the shelves. When I find it, I pull it off the shelf and hold it out to her. "It's a novel in verse. Beautifully written. Caroline-Kate St. Pucella's poems are incredible."

"I haven't heard of them before," Ramona admits. She considers the book for a moment before saying, "I'll have to check this out."

We don't talk for a few minutes, mostly because I'm not sure what to say. I want to tell her that her so-called friends are kind of the worst, but I'm not sure how she'd take that. I don't know if I would've listened if someone had told me about Nikki's true personality.

"Thanks," Ramona eventually says, holding up the book. She glances around and then asks, "Do you, uh, work here or something?"

I almost laugh, a smile spreading across my face. "No, I just . . . read a lot?"

Ramona does laugh.

Feeling a little courageous, I add, "Back at my old school . . . I had a friend who kind of reminds me of Alexandra."

Ramona's eyebrows come together. "What . . . What do you mean?"

"I don't know what I mean. Never mind." The courage seems to dry up.

Ramona looks down at the book in her hand and then back to me. "Tell me."

I swallow. "I guess I just mean that she reminds me of the way my friend would sort of . . . make me feel bad."

She stares at me, her expression very neutral. "Are you trying to imply something?"

I panic, and I want to take back the words. Maybe she has no idea how bad Alexandra is.

"Nothing. Just . . . nothing," I sputter. When I catch sight of the board game display, all I can say next is "Do you want to play a game? Uncle Moe has some over there and—"

Ramona seems to consider my offer. After a long moment of silence, she says, "Sure," like it's no big deal. I'm surprised, confused, and relieved all at once.

"Really?" I ask.

"Why not?" Ramona says, shrugging.

I show her to my table and offer to get us a game. I'm browsing the shelf when I hear Kevin's voice: "Eden's at the back."

Ducking around the games display, I peek to see Duke coming my way. *Oh no.* If he sees Ramona . . .

I rush around the display to meet him awkwardly in the middle of the aisle.

"Duke! Hi! Are you looking for me?"

Duke tilts his head, smiling. "Yeah. I came to pick up that book I ordered—you know, the one you recommended—and thought I'd say a quick hello if you were here. I texted you, but you didn't respond."

"That's so nice," I blurt. "My phone is in my backpack on silent, so I didn't see it. Uh, is your mom waiting for you?"

"Brother," he answers. "Um. Edie, is everything okay? You're acting a little . . . jumpy."

"Jumpy how?"

"I don't know . . . just . . ." Duke gestures with his hand. He frowns at my sweater pocket. "Isn't that your phone?"

I look down at my sweater, where my phone pulls the pocket down a bit. *Crap.* "Oh! Silly me. I guess it isn't in my backpack." Duke looks around, trying to see behind me. Then he frowns and I know he's seen her purple-and-pink hair. "Is that Ramona?"

"Uh. No!" I lie.

"That's definitely Ramona Augustus. Are . . . Are you *here* with her?" Duke takes a step forward.

Instinctively I stick my hand out and stop him from going around me.

"No," I lie again. "I'm sitting over by the windows. I didn't—I didn't, uh, see her there."

Duke doesn't look like he believes me, but then he quietly says, "Okay, good. You know she's not to be trusted."

"Right." I glance down before asking, "Why, again?"

"Just trust me," Duke says. "I gotta go, but Eden. You do *not* want to be friends with Ramona, okay?"

"Okay," I whisper. "I'll see you tomorrow?"

"Yeah," he says. He gives me a quick hug and holds up the book. "Thanks again for the recommendation."

I nod, watching him leave.

"Is everything okay?"

I almost scream at the sound of Ramona's voice. I spin around and let out a breath. "Yeah, sorry. I—I got distracted. Want to help me find a game?"

"Sure," Ramona says.

And I can't help but wonder if Duke would still be my friend knowing that I just lied to his face. I feel sick to my stomach. He *trusts* me. He believed my obvious lie. It takes everything in me not to burst into tears.

16

On Friday, my leg bounces up and down a mile a minute. I didn't expect Jackie and Tabitha to sit with me in class, but they do. Normally I spend some time writing in my journal, but it's kind of nice how natural it feels to be sitting with them.

Tabitha is busy folding an origami hummingbird again, Jackie is waving their hand around to correct our history teacher on Christopher Columbus and *exactly* who he was, and me? I'm sitting here wondering if Ms. Barnes is going to make us do the new assignment in a group or individually. I'd prefer to do it alone . . . I think? I'm not sure. It might be—and I don't want to get ahead of myself here—*fun* to work with my friends on it.

My friends.

Who I still haven't invited to my birthday party.

What if we're not friends by then? What if they get bored of me? It's not like that hasn't happened before. Nikki told me as much—she didn't find me "interesting enough."

I can still hear her exact words. *No offense, Eden, but you're not interesting enough to be nonbinary—not that that's a real thing.*

Panic bubbles up in my chest, but then Jackie starts waving their hand around in the air with more urgency and it catches my attention.

Breathe. Inhale . . . two, three, four, hold . . . two, three, four . . . exhale, two, three, four . . .

"Yes, Jackie?" Ms. Barnes finally relents. The sound of her voice snaps me out of my breathing, but by now, I'm feeling calmer.

"You've got it all wrong, Ms. Barnes. Because Columbus was *awful* to Indigenous people. He wasn't some sort of hero," Jackie says. "In fact, he was a *terrible* explorer. But objectively he was a bad man. Why are we learning about him?"

"Let's discuss this more after class," Ms. Barnes says, and I can tell she's a little rattled. I would be too if a student knew more than I did as a teacher.

"But—" Jackie starts again.

"*After* class, Jackie," Ms. Barnes says with a sterner look now.

Someone else raises their hand and the conversation—and focus—moves on.

"Does anyone know the answer?" Ms. Barnes asks about five minutes later. "Eden?"

I freeze at the sound of my name. I haven't been paying attention. I was trying to fold another hummingbird on my own. "Um."

"I do!" Duke interjects from his seat. "The ships he used were caravels."

118

I let out the smallest breath of relief.

"Thank you, Duke. Next time, I would like *Eden* to answer," Ms. Barnes says.

I'm grateful when she continues on, ignoring me, until she announces: "This weekly assignment will be done in groups of four or five. Find your group now."

This is usually where I wait until after class to say I don't have a group and I'd like to do it alone. But today is different. Jackie swings around to look at me, and Tabitha shifts in her seat.

"What do you say?" Jackie asks.

"Definitely a group," Tabitha says. She waves over to Duke, who is sitting beside Benji. "Duke, come be with us. You're always with them."

"Sure," Duke says easily. He turns to Benji and Trey to say, "You heard her. I'm with them on this project. That cool?"

"Whatever," Benji replies.

My lips part, but no words come out.

I, Eden Jones, have a group project . . . with *friends*. This has never happened before.

Tabitha finishes her hummingbird and hands it to me. Quietly she says, "Don't look so concerned. We'll work hard and get a decent grade."

I almost laugh. "Don't worry, I wasn't thinking about my grade."

"I was wondering if you all want to come to my house next Saturday," Duke says.

"Yes" is the immediate answer from the three of us.

"Figured we could go in the hot tub and stuff, so bring your bathing suits," he adds.

"Ooh, I *love* hot tubs," Jackie says, rubbing their hands together.

We're sitting in a group of four, discussing how we can talk about the *real* events of Christopher Columbus according to Jackie, when the classroom door swings open. Ramona Augustus slips into the room and looks around.

"Ugh," Duke mumbles, "I hope Ms. Barnes doesn't put her with us."

"Miss Augustus, please join a group with four people in it," Ms. Barnes instructs.

Ramona looks over to her friends, the volleyball girls, but they're a group of five. They give her an apologetic look but turn away a second later.

And I wonder . . . Is it possible to be surrounded by people and still feel just as lonely?

I glance back to where Ramona stands awkwardly at the front of the classroom, looking around, desperate to make eye contact with *anyone*.

I've been her, I realize. After Nikki and I stopped being friends, before I moved to Middleton . . . I was standing all alone at the front of the classroom while the teacher had to assign me to a group. No one wanted me.

I stick my hand in the air and wave for her to come join us. I know Duke might hate me for this, but I can't leave her up there alone.

"What are you doing?" Duke hisses.

Ramona's eyebrows raise and her jaw slackens slightly. Then she adjusts her backpack and walks over to us.

"I can't believe you just—Ramona! Hi," Duke says when she reaches us.

She presses her lips together before saying, "Hi . . . Duke."

I watch them. Jackie and Tabitha stare at me with wide eyes, and I have a feeling what I did was worse than I thought. I'm not sure what it was, but I mouth a silent "sorry" to Duke. He doesn't want me to trust Ramona, but . . . he's wrong about her. I know it.

Duke sighs and pushes his textbook aside on the desk. "You're welcome to join us."

Ramona's face is filled with tentative relief as she takes a seat. She bites her bottom lip before asking, "What's the project?"

"Here," Jackie says, jumping at the chance to hand the assignment paper to Ramona. "We're going to focus on Christopher Columbus."

"Ugh, *that* guy?" Ramona says.

I try to hide my smile when Jackie's face lights up. They launch into how they want us to approach the project: not shying away from the truth. Duke gives me a look with his lips pressed tight together, and the guilt seeps into my skin.

What if he doesn't forgive me for this?

My mind races. *What if Duke never truly gets over what I've done? What if he stays annoyed at me and it builds and builds until he can't stand to see my face anymore? What if they all find out the truth? What if I'm not worthy of their friendship because all I've been doing is lying?*

What if . . . what if . . . what if . . . It's all my mind can think.

17

ME: hey I'm hanging out with my friends after school today

MOM: Okay, have fun sweetheart! 😊🫶💜

We don't have much time in class to go over the logistics of who is going to tackle which part of the history project, so we agree to meet after school. Duke says he promised to play some basketball down at the community center, and everyone decides we'll just watch his pickup game and then figure out the project afterward.

Benji and Trey offer for us to join the basketball game, and even have some extra pinnies for us. I shake my head no, stepping backward out of defense. Jackie and Tabitha opt not to play too. Ramona, on the other hand, holds her hands out for a pinny.

Trey tosses one at her, and she pulls it on without a word. I watch her jog onto the basketball court, and Duke gives me a *look*. There's no mistaking what that look is for either. He's annoyed at me.

He didn't talk to me the entire way here; he stayed up with Jackie and Tabitha. I hung back with Ramona. We didn't say much to each other—well, we said nothing to each other, really.

"I can't believe you waved Ramona over," Jackie hisses to me as we walk over to the bleachers.

"Yeah, Eden, what *was* that?" Tabitha asks.

My lips part but I don't say anything. Not until we're sitting down, huddled near the top of the bleachers. I swallow, but there's a knot in my throat. A pit in my stomach. "I'm not sure I understand what the big deal is."

Jackie lets out a low whistle.

"I wish I could whistle," Tabitha comments before straightening up. "Wait, you don't *know*?"

"I've only been here for, like, a month and a half," I point out. I tug on my sweater, pulling it closer to me. "What's the big deal?"

This is unfair of me—I knew there was *something* between Duke and Ramona.

I pull on the sleeves of my sweater to wrap them around my hands, which curl into fists.

Jackie bites down on their lip. "I don't know if it's really our business. I'm surprised that Duke didn't tell you, though."

Well, he sort of did.

"Let's just say . . . Duke and Ramona used to be best friends."

"Oh," I whisper.

I look out over the basketball court. Duke and Ramona are on different teams, and I wonder if that was done on purpose.

If someone had done to me with Nikki Gladstone what I had just done to Duke . . . I wouldn't be happy with myself either.

"Yeah." Jackie nudges me with their elbow. I almost jump at the contact. "It's cool, though. I'm sure Duke knows you didn't mean anything by it."

Right.

I watch as Duke darts around Ramona, shoots, and the ball goes straight into the basket. His team cheers, but he doesn't celebrate. Instead, he brushes past Ramona as they reset.

I wonder if maybe I read Ramona wrong. If she wronged Duke . . .

But my gut screams *She's just lonely like me!* And I don't know what to listen to.

I chew on my bottom lip, wondering how I could've messed up so badly.

Please don't leave me now, I silently beg Duke as if he can hear my thoughts. *I need you.*

"You know," Jackie says, leaning back calmly, as though I didn't just completely screw up everything, "I know nothing about sports, and I'm going to keep it that way."

Tabitha laughs. I roll my shoulders, but the tension doesn't leave them.

"It's probably the last time they'll be able to play outside before it gets too cold, you think?" Tabitha asks, rubbing her hands together. "So, we should enjoy it while we can."

"Okay, but so far, this is boring," Jackie whispers.

Mostly we sit in silence, bundled up. Jackie huddles closer to me, and Tabitha keeps rubbing her hands together. I tug my scarf up to cover my nose.

Jackie starts clapping when Duke gets a three-pointer. I do a silent cheer with my hands for him, and startle when Jackie jumps to their feet, shouting, "LET'S GOOO, DUKE!"

Then Ramona steals the ball from Duke, and they sit down with a huff. "Dang. Okay, maybe this sport-watching thing isn't so bad."

Tabitha laughs. "So much for this being boring, huh?"

Jackie sticks their tongue out in response. I smile nervously beneath my scarf. I tuck my hands between my thick thighs to keep them warm.

When the teams take a break, I want to go talk to Duke. But I'm afraid, so I stay in my seat. Ramona jogs over to us to grab her water bottle from her backpack. We make eye contact—only briefly—and then she looks away.

Usually it's me looking away first.

"The guys are going to play another game," Duke says when he reaches us. He doesn't look at me, though; instead he keeps his eyes on Jackie and Tabitha. "Let's get to work, I guess."

He's still mad at me. I know it.

"Sure," Ramona says, nodding.

"Sounds good," Jackie adds, pulling out their binder from their backpack.

I feel my chest tighten, but I'm not sure what I can do right now. I feel frozen. The sounds of the boys playing basketball are louder than before, and the wind whips through the court with a furious anger. My cheeks are red from the cold.

Time seems to slow down.

I think I'm having a panic attack, I realize belatedly. It's happening all too fast. I can't stop it.

Suddenly I can't see anything. It's all a blur. I can't focus on the things in front of me. Can't hear anything well—it sounds like it's in the distance. Can't feel my hands.

I'm completely still.

Alone.

And then someone grabs my shoulder and starts shaking me. "Eden? Eden, can you hear me?"

I can't respond. My breath quickens. My chest is tight. I feel dizzy.

"What's happening?" I hear someone's voice. Tabitha, maybe? No, no—Jackie. It's too loud to be Tabitha. "What's going on? Eden?"

"Eden, I need you to breathe. Slowly," Duke says. "Can you do that for me?"

I blink, and it's like time catches up with me. Slows down. Speeds up. I'm not sure. But I'm being slightly jerked back and forth by Duke.

Coughing, I roll my shoulders to let him know I'm back. I'm in my body . . . I think. Everything feels fuzzy, but I manage to reach one hand up and put it on Duke's. He stops shaking me.

"Eden?" he asks, and his voice is thick with worry.

"Ye-yeah," I manage. I look up at him. "Sorry, I . . . I just . . ."

"Had a panic attack?" Duke asks, his voice soft.

"Yeah." I let out a shaky breath. "Thanks, Duke."

I look around, and Ramona stands behind him, eyes wide. Duke grabs both my hands in his and asks, "You okay? You really freaked me out there. You weren't responding."

"I just . . . froze," I mumble. Things are starting to become clearer now. I can focus on the basketball bros. They paused playing to see what's going on. Jackie's concerned voice probably carried across the court.

My worst nightmare.

The panic starts to bubble again, but then I hear Tabitha say, "Eden, it's okay. We're just worried about you . . . No one's judging you."

I manage to look at her for a second and it doesn't sound like she's lying.

"Eden's fine!" Duke calls out to his friends.

"You sure?" Trey calls back.

Duke gives them a thumbs-up and then focuses on me. "See,

they're just playing basketball now. What . . . What happened?"

Tears well up in my eyes, and I hate that everyone is about to see me cry. I'd run, but I don't think my legs are working yet.

"I don't know. I didn't even notice it building," I say. I look at him because he's the only one I feel completely safe with right now. His brother gets panic attacks. He knows what this is like.

I realize I'm shaking when Jackie wraps their scarf around my neck, over my own scarf.

"You're okay, okay?" Duke says and lets out a soft breath. "You really freaked me out there, Edie."

"I didn't—I didn't mean to," I mumble.

"I know," he says, squeezing my hand tight in his.

"Thank you," I whisper. He was there for me, even though he's mad at me. I thought I messed everything up with Duke, but he didn't even hesitate to help me.

"C'mon, let's *all* go to Uncle Moe's, get some hot chocolate, and just chill. We can figure out the history project later, right, guys?" Duke asks.

"Right!" I hear an echo of voices around me.

I nod.

"Yeah. Sounds . . . good."

Duke helps me up, hands my backpack to Tabitha, hooks my arm in his, and doesn't let me go the entire walk to Uncle Moe's.

18

"You're quiet tonight," Mom comments as she piles mashed potatoes onto her plate. She pauses with a spoonful midair to give me a look. "Everything okay?"

"Yeah," I say. "Just a little drained from the basketball game earlier."

"Did you play?"

I snort. "No. Duke and Ramona did, though. His team won, and he even scored the final points!" It feels weird telling her the truth about what I did. I can say these things to her and *mean* them. At the realization, my throat thickens, and I stare down at my meal.

"That's great," Mom says, smiling.

"Yeah."

I could tell her about the panic attack I had, and how Duke was there for me. But I don't really want to worry her . . . and I don't really know where Duke and I stand. The panic attack changed the vibes, but I still messed up. I shouldn't have risked my friendship with Duke to include Ramona. At least, I should've asked him about including her first.

We went to Uncle Moe's for hot chocolate and cookies as Duke suggested, and it was hard—extra hard because Ramona was there.

I was tense for almost an hour after my panic attack. I think I owe Duke an apology, but I don't even know where to start.

It's a little hard to keep track of all I'm feeling these days, so I wrote some of the moments down in my journal when I got home, like how I love when Duke can't stop laughing and it keeps going and going until everyone else is laughing too. And how Jackie is obsessed with older music like Britney Spears and Jesse McCartney—they even admitted to having dance parties in their bedroom. And how Ramona was quiet but still participated with softer answers than I expected. And how Tabitha really hates her name, but when we asked her what she'd prefer to be known as, she said she didn't know yet. *Tabitha or Tabs is fine*, she said, *but thanks for offering to call me something else.*

It was a nice moment, so I scribbled it down in my journal, hoping to always remember it.

"Where'd you go, Eden?" Mom asks.

I blink, looking up. "Oh. Um. Nowhere. It was just a good day, that's all."

"I'm glad. You've seemed . . . happier lately," Mom says before shoving a forkful of potatoes into her mouth. She squeals and tries to say "Hot! Hot! Hot!"

I laugh and she gives me a pained look before downing some water.

"You know, I have to say, I really think changing schools was great for you," Mom tells me a moment later. I look up to meet her eyes. "You're glowing these days. I think these friends of yours are good ones."

"Yeah?" I ask, despite myself.

"Yeah. I mean, you've been happier, more social than *ever* before. I barely saw you last week."

"You were working!" I jokingly protest.

Mom laughs. "Still, you had plans like . . . every night. I'm just happy to see how far you've come, Eden. I really think it's only the beginning for you."

"Thanks, Mom." But the guilt comes back in one big swoop: How am I going to pull this off? What if Duke doesn't forgive me about Ramona? What if I can't get either of them to come to my party after all?

After dinner I help her load the dishwasher, and a question keeps circling back to me. "Mom?"

"Yeah, kid?" she asks from the kitchen table.

I close the dishwasher. *How would you feel if you knew I'd been lying about having friends for over a month now? How angry and hurt and confused would you be? Would you hate me? Would you look at me the way you looked at Dad?*

"Never mind. I'm going to go do some homework."

"Okay." Mom kisses my forehead and then I jog up the stairs to my bedroom.

I run my hand along the hallway wall, my mind filled with memories of how excited Mom was when the mortgage was approved. She worked hard to get this house for us, working two jobs at once to save up enough money.

I shut the bedroom door behind me. This place feels more permanent. I *have* to make it work. I think I can get my friends here for the birthday party . . . but what about after the party ends?

Even though, right now, it *feels* like I have friends. Real friends. Friends who care about me. And maybe even *four* of them. That is, if Duke forgives me. And Ramona hangs out with us again. And that's okay with Duke.

Ugh. Everything's so complicated now.

I settle onto my bed with my textbook and homework. Not only do I struggle to get my work done with all the socializing I've been doing, but I also haven't had a lot of time to journal.

I write as much down as I can think of until I struggle to keep my eyes open. But I know my next steps: apologize to Duke, figure out the Ramona situation, and maybe . . . Maybe it's time to ask them to my party.

19

"What are you writing?" Jackie asks, peering over. I snap my journal shut. They immediately hold their hands up. "Whoa, sorry."

I scrunch up my nose. "No, I'm sorry. It's just my journal."

"Gotcha," Jackie says. They lean back and let out a heavy sigh. "I'm bored."

"What?" Duke says, surprised. "This is, like, *your* assignment. Aren't you excited to present how much the textbooks are missing?"

"I know, but . . . Christopher Columbus was a terrible person and it's depressing." Jackie frowns. "I just need a mental break."

I almost laugh. I need the same.

"Fair enough," Tabitha says, closing her laptop. "I'm done for today too."

"Should, um, should I go, then?" Ramona asks, standing up. But her eyes are searching Duke's face.

"Do what you want," Duke says without looking up from his laptop. "I'm not your keeper."

Ramona closes her eyes, takes a few deep breaths, and says, "Duke, I'm *trying*."

"Trying to do what, exactly?" he demands, closing his laptop with force.

My eyes bounce between them, and my chest tightens. I hate conflict. "Um, Duke, Ramona—"

"Trying to be nice!" Ramona says, her voice rising a little.

"Oh, sure. *You*, nice?" Duke scoffs.

"Please—"

"Don't," Duke says, snapping at me. He meets my eyes. "Eden, you've done enough. This is between me and Ramona."

She rolls her eyes.

"Real nice," Duke says, pressing his lips together.

"Sorry, it's just, you're *impossible*."

"*I'm* impossible?" Duke asks, jerking back. "I've been *nothing* but nice to you."

"Please!" I shout. I glance around, but I don't think anyone else in Uncle Moe's heard me. I take a breath and quietly say, "Can't we just get along?"

Duke glares at Ramona for a moment before saying to me, "Eden, you don't understand."

He's right. I don't.

"You don't need to be friends," I say, feeling a little brave. "But we *do* have an assignment together. So, you need to figure out how to be around each other without fighting."

"I can do that," Ramona says.

We all wait for Duke's response. Finally he shrugs. "Whatever. Stay if you want. I don't care."

Ramona hesitates before sitting back down in her chair.

Jackie and Tabitha share looks with me, but I'm just as lost. *What happened between them?* Suddenly I feel a need to fill the silence that falls over the table.

"You know, two of my friends at my old school used to fight a lot," I lie. "They both liked the same boy."

"The friend who reminded you of me?" Tabitha asks, keeping her tone light and careful.

"Yeah," I say, because it's easy.

"I would never," Tabitha says, shaking her head.

I snort, because of course she wouldn't. She's a lesbian. But Ramona doesn't know that. Duke laughs, and Jackie lets out a deep breath. Ramona looks around at each of us.

"What am I missing?" she asks.

"I'm a lesbian," Tabitha says, eyes focused on Ramona's reaction. Her expression is like she's . . . *testing* Ramona. And I think Ramona understands that.

"So, you quite literally would never fight over a boy." Then she laughs, saying, "That's really funny, actually!" A moment later she adds, "Thanks for letting me in on the joke."

I see Tabitha's shoulders drop in relief, but Duke seems tense still.

"Do you have a problem with Tabitha?" Duke demands, sounding harsher than I've ever heard him before. He doesn't tear his eyes away from Ramona, and his gaze is hard and challenging.

I fidget with my hands in my lap, glancing around the table. Jackie makes a little o with their lips, Tabitha raises an eyebrow, and Ramona lifts her chin slightly. She meets Duke's eyes and holds his gaze when she says, "No. I do not."

"Good." Duke shifts on his chair and looks away from her, but I catch Ramona watching him carefully.

"I'm pansexual," Ramona explains. "I think. I don't know."

"What?" Duke says, his eyes snapping back to Ramona.

"It's nothing, it's—"

Duke looks at me, eyes wide, and I wish I understood what exactly happened between them. I'm starting to think I might never know . . . if I don't ask. But I don't know how to ask.

"It's not nothing," Jackie says, reaching their hand out to make their point. "But it's also okay if you're not sure."

"Thanks," Ramona mumbles, looking shy.

"Jackie's right." This comes from Duke, and I think he surprises himself the most.

My fidgeting becomes a little more intense. I have no idea what to do right now. I want to run, but that'd be rude, so I stay put.

The tension in the air is thick.

My chest tightens.

"Do you want to talk about it?" Duke asks, sounding almost cautious. Like he's afraid to spook Ramona.

"Um. Not really. No."

There's a heavy silence.

I'm itching to break it somehow. I don't realize what I'm saying until I've said, "Will y'all come to my birthday party in a few weeks?"

Everyone looks at me. I want to hide my face, but I'm frozen. I don't know if I've ever had so many people see me at the same time.

Then they all start talking at once.

Duke: "What! I had no idea your birthday was coming up, dude!"

Tabitha: "Of course."

Jackie: "Y'all?"

Ramona: "What?"

"We need more information," Duke says, gesturing his hand widely.

"Um. It's like, three weekends from Saturday?" I manage. "In the middle of November. Saturday, November sixteenth."

"Well, count me in," Duke tells me. Jackie and Tabitha nod.

Ramona bends down to grab her backpack and says, "Well, if we're not going to—"

"You're invited too," I interrupt.

Ramona, please, I silently beg. *I need you there. I promised my mom.*

"Why me?" she asks bluntly. "I don't really get it."

"Me neither," Duke mutters. I elbow him in the side, and he winces. "Eden!"

"Look, I don't know what your deal with each other is, but I would like it if you put your differences aside and come to my party."

There. I said it. I said what I need from them. I feel sick.

"Um," Ramona murmurs. She looks helplessly at Duke, who shrugs.

"Whatever," Duke mutters. "Ramona can come if she wants. I don't care."

"I'd—I'd like to," Ramona continues. She sets down her backpack and lets out a deep breath. "But I want to know something first. Why did you try to talk to me after class the other week, Eden?"

"Yeah," Duke says. "*Why* did you?"

I look between them both and stay silent. I think I told Duke some story about her knowing my cousin, which he definitely just figured out was a lie.

I don't really know what to say to that. It's not as if I can tell them all that I *need* them to come to my birthday party—to keep up a lie that I've been telling my mom.

"I . . . I . . . I just wanted to be Ramona's friend, I guess," is all I can think to say.

I don't dare look at Duke.

"Honestly I'm actually a little relieved to be hanging out with you all," Ramona says, her voice quiet. "It's a change of pace from the volleyball girls."

"They're kind of awful," Jackie comments.

"They're not all bad," Ramona responds. "I mean, Alexandra is a bit tough on people, but she's got a good heart at the end of the day."

"Sure," Tabitha scoffs. "She's probably the meanest of all."

"Definitely," Duke agrees, and Ramona's eyes flash to his. He looks away, though, and I wonder if Alexandra is part of the reason they aren't friends anymore.

"I don't know about that . . ." Ramona trails off as if she's not even sure herself.

There's silence again, but I'm not the one to break it. That comes from Tabitha, who asks, "So, Eden, what would you like for your birthday?"

"Books with queer joy, *obviously*," Jackie says dramatically.

We laugh, and the tension seems to be broken for now.

"Is that all you read?" Ramona asks, glancing at me.

"Mostly," I say with a shrug. "There's something freeing about seeing people just like you in books."

"Can I ask something?" Tabitha says. "It's kind of personal, so you don't need to answer."

"Sure," I say tentatively.

"How did you know you weren't cis?"

Jackie, Duke, and I all share looks.

"Um," I start.

"I can answer that," Jackie says. Ramona looks mildly surprised. "I'm genderqueer, and my pronouns are they/he."

Duke looks on edge until Ramona takes a deep breath, nods, and says, "Okay."

"Anyway, I was always playing dress-up in my parents' closet. Trying on their clothes, trying to figure out what suited me best. I really like to blur the lines of gendered clothing, and I'd always shop in both the girls' and boys' sections at stores. No one in my family thinks it's weird because I've been doing it for as long as I can remember . . . They don't know I'm genderqueer, but I really don't think it'd be a surprise to them."

"It was, like, gender expression that helped you figure it out?" Tabitha asks.

"One hundred percent," Jackie confirms with a nod. "I think playing with gender expression is fun. Helps me express how I really feel, you know?"

"What about you, Duke?" This question comes from Ramona, who bites down on her bottom lip. She doesn't look up at us, just stares down at her half-eaten muffin on the table. "How . . . How did you know?"

Duke glances at me like he's unsure if he should answer. I give him a tiny but encouraging nod to go ahead. His hand suddenly touches mine under the table. If this is what he needs right now, so be it.

"Because," he whispers, voice thick. "I realized I could never truly be a volleyball girl like you."

Ramona's eyes flicker, but her expression is hard to read. I have no idea what she's thinking so I give Duke's hand a squeeze.

Jackie plays with their water bottle label, and Tabitha keeps her eyes on the bottle too. I don't know where to look or what to think.

I almost jump when Ramona grabs her backpack this time. "Sorry. I shouldn't have—"

Duke's hand slips out of mine as he reaches out. "I'm *trying* here, Mona."

Mona? I don't think I've ever heard anyone call Ramona by a nickname before. I scrunch my face up at the realization that I really have no idea what their history is and I'm the reason they're having this tough conversation in front of everyone right now.

Ramona doesn't stop this time, though. She stands up and says, "I'm—I—I have to go."

"Wait!"

The word explodes from me.

I don't mean it to.

But I saw the look of devastation on Duke's face.

Ramona mouths "sorry" before darting through the aisles until she's out of sight.

What have I done?

"Duke—"

"It's fine, Eden."

"But—"

"Really," he says, looking at me. "The stuff between Ramona and me isn't your fault. It's complicated and . . . I'm surprised she even *asked*. I'm not surprised she ran. She always runs."

There's another silence, and this time, it feels like it's choking me. I don't know what to do. I don't want to lose Duke. This is all my fault.

I inhale sharply and say, "I don't know what happened with you two, but I'm *sorry*."

"I think that's the first time you've said that," Duke mutters. He looks at me with a hard expression. "It's really crappy that you didn't listen to me when I told you that Ramona isn't to be trusted."

"What happened?" I whisper.

Tabitha and Jackie look at each other and Duke stares down at the laptop in front of him. "I don't feel like talking about it, okay? This whole situation sucks."

"It does. I'm sorry, really. I shouldn't have done that," I tell him. "Do . . . Do you hate me?"

Duke lets out a breath. "No. I'm just going to be annoyed with you for a little while."

"Okay," I say, nodding. "Am, um, am I still invited to your house on Saturday?"

Duke rolls his eyes. "Of course."

I let out the breath that caught in my throat.

20

"I think this is the first time I've dropped you off at Duke's," Mom says, glancing over at me. "It seems pretty far to walk . . . How do you usually get here?"

"Bus," I say quickly. Although, that would require her to write me a permission slip more often than not. And I don't know if the public bus comes this way. Quickly I add, "But usually Duke's older brother gives us a ride."

"All of you?" Mom asks. And I'm panicking. There wouldn't be enough room for us in his truck. But . . .

"He takes their mom's van."

Does Duke's mom even own a van? I don't know. But it sounds good. I nod more to myself for coming up with the lie so quickly and shoot her a quick glance.

Mom considers this. "Oh. I guess you gotta do what you gotta do."

"Yeah," I say softly. *Please don't push for more answers*, I silently beg.

"Nice neighborhood," Mom comments as we turn down his road. I carefully and subtly check my messages for the house number again. "Which one is Duke's?"

"Oh, uh," I say, trying to get a good look at the numbers on the side of the houses. *Crap.* "We've passed it."

"We have?" Mom asks, frowning. "I'm surprised you didn't realize if you've been here a bunch."

"Wasn't paying attention?" I half lie as she turns around in someone's driveway. A moment later I say, "Oh, it's right there!"

Being at Duke's house means meeting his parents and older brother. I'm terrified of meeting new people. I've never met someone's entire family before, so I'm extra nervous.

I'm bracing myself for a panic attack when Mom pulls up to Duke's house.

"Thanks, Mom. I'll text you when you can pick me up. Or I can get a ride—"

"I'll pick you up. Have fun. Love you!" Mom says, blowing me a kiss.

"Love you."

I get out of the car and head toward the front door. Before I even make it to the front steps, the door swings open and Duke stands there. A weight is lifted off my chest. No matter what, Duke will protect me. I believe that much. Even if he has no idea *why* I invited him to my birthday party.

"Hey," he says without excitement. He's probably still mad at me. He's been busy with the basketball boys lately, so I feel like I haven't seen him much. I wince.

"I know I'm a little early but . . ." *But this way, I can meet people slowly. Hopefully.*

"Don't worry about it. I asked Mom to go get some snacks for us. So it's just my dad and my brother here right now. Dad is in his office, so you might meet him later." Duke shrugs. "I looked up what to do if your friend has Social Anxiety Disorder, and it recommended meeting new people one-on-one."

I run at Duke, throwing my backpack onto the ground, and wrap my arms around him. It's probably our first *real* hug. It takes him a moment, but then he wraps his arms around me, and we're hugging, and it's just . . .

It's overwhelming.

"Duke, you are my best friend," I tell him when I pull away, keeping my hands on his arms. I feel my eyes start to water. I can't believe I'm about to cry in front of Duke. I take a deep, but shaky, breath and hold the tears back the best I can. "Thank you. I was so worried about this, and I'm *so* sorry. I should've never done that to you, sprung her on you like that, and . . . and, and—"

"Hey, hey, it's okay." Duke gives me his bright smile and his eyes shine. "It was crappy, but . . . I've had some time to think. You don't know the whole story, so you don't really *get* it. But I still got you, Edie."

My face softens, with warm cheeks, when I pick up my backpack and enter Duke's house. I look around and suppress the attempt to whistle. It's nice but not too nice—I already feel like this is a *home*.

"Wow, I like your place."

"Huh? Oh, thanks," he says. There's a knock at the door. "Oh, that must be Jackie or Tabs."

Duke swings the front door open again and gives Tabitha a big smile. *Bigger than I got.* "Hey! You made it!"

"Hey," Tabitha says, looking a little sad. "I've got some news, but I'll wait until Jack gets here too."

"Jack? We're calling Jackie Jack now?" I ask.

"Don't worry, you're still Edie to me," Duke sings, smirking. I roll my eyes. "I think that's Jackie coming up the path now."

We all peer out and let them into the house. We hover awkwardly after our greetings, and then Tabitha asks if we can go somewhere private to talk.

Duke takes us upstairs to his bedroom. It's a typical guy bedroom, with blue walls, a blue comforter, and a wall of trophies. A little messy, but I can tell he tried to clean up.

"What's going on?" Duke asks Tabitha after we've all fully inspected his stuff.

"My foster mom's dad is ill, so he has to move into my room. Meaning they don't have space for me anymore."

"But they made a commitment!" Duke argues.

"I know, but things happen." Tabitha pulls her sweater close. "They already have four biological kids, so it's pretty cramped anyway."

"Where are you going?" Jackie asks, concerned.

I'm trying to process the news.

"My social worker said they don't have another family for me, so I'm going to a group home. It's whatever. But it *might* mean that I'll no longer be in the school district." Tabitha takes a deep breath before telling us in simple English: "It means that I might not be going to Middleton anymore."

"What! No!" I protest along with Duke and Jackie. I continue, "You can't leave. We just found each other. And you're one of us."

"Ha. Tell that to the universe," Tabitha says, pacing the room. "I just . . . I don't know what I'm going to do."

Tabitha's eyes start tearing up. I'm not sure what to do, but Duke and Jackie share a look. Jackie reaches out and grabs one of Tabitha's hands.

"It's going to be okay, Tabs. Whatever happens, we'll figure it out together."

"Yeah, what are friends for?" Duke jokes.

"I'm so sorry," I whisper to Tabitha. She sniffs but nods.

"It's okay. It'll be okay," she says.

"How?" Duke asks, and the word echoes around his bedroom.

I pick at a loose thread on Duke's comforter, trying to think of something—anything—I can do to make it better.

"How about we go into the hot tub and come up with ideas?" Duke asks, falling back onto the bed with me.

"Ideas?" Tabitha asks, looking around at us. "Ideas for what?"

"For getting you to stay," Duke says as if it's obvious. I didn't quite get that either, but I nod as if I did.

I give him a quick smile, but it falls fast. I have no idea what we could do.

We take turns changing into our bathing suits in the bathroom, and while Tabitha waits in the hall for Jackie to finish, I find myself alone with Duke in his bedroom.

He shuffles on his feet, and I notice his expression change. "You were with Ramona that day I picked up my book."

Startled, I bite my bottom lip. There are two options: Be honest or lie again. I don't want to lie to Duke anymore. So I say "Yes."

Duke nods, taking this information in.

"I'm sorry," I blurt, panicking. "I shouldn't have lied, but I knew you wouldn't approve, and—"

"I can't believe you!" Duke says, shaking his head. "Seriously, Eden. Why lie?"

Oof. That's a heavy question. I swallow hard and wish I could just come clean about everything. The lies to Mom, the fake friendships from my old school, everything. But I can't seem to bring myself to say anything like that. Instead, I say, "I'm sorry. I'm really sorry, Duke. I knew that you had some stuff with Ramona, and I . . . I didn't want you to find out."

Duke sighs. "Well, what's done is done. Just . . . Don't lie to me again, okay?"

I want to make sure I never lie to Duke again, but I'm worried that the truth will only push him away.

"Okay."

"Because that sucks."

"Okay," I echo. My heart pounds hard. *Now what?*

I look at his wall of photos with all his basketball bros and wonder what it's like to be part of a team. A group of people who will have your back, who you work with, and who build you up to be better.

I find myself longing for what Duke has—an easy relationship with everyone in his life. I swallow and look over some more photos. I don't face him when I say, "You look happy in these photos."

"I was." Duke walks over to join me, nudging me with his arm. I don't know why he does it, but when I glance at him, I feel a little tension evaporate. "But I struggled to feel like I belonged too."

"You did?" Startled, I look back at the team photos. "But you're in the center of almost all these photos."

"Yeah, but . . . Well, you get it." Duke gestures wildly. "It took me a

151

long time to feel like I belonged. I felt like an outsider for being trans."

"Oh." I look closer. "You're only on boys' teams in these photos."

"Yeah. I used to be on the girls' teams for sports, but . . ."

"You're a boy," I say, nodding. I get that. I'm nonbinary. I don't fit into the idea of the gender binary. The world is so set on pinks and blues, and I'm yellow, green, and orange. "Was it hard?"

Duke nods. "Yeah. The volleyball girls don't talk to me anymore."

I can't picture Duke being one of the volleyball girls; he might have a bit of a rough edge to him, but he's so kind and gracious to the world and the people around him.

But then it hits me, and I turn to face him. "Ramona?"

"Yeah. She was my best friend." Duke shrugs. "I don't really get what happened. She just . . . let our friendship end suddenly, and wordlessly, after I came out. Like, she couldn't even look at me."

"Duke, I—" But I don't know what to say. *I'm so sorry*, my mind screams, but the words are caught in my throat.

"It's chill, Eden," he says. He sets a photo of him on the boys' basketball team down onto the desk. "You really didn't know."

"Still . . . It sucks she abandoned you." I close my eyes and let out a breath. "And that I brought her back into your life."

"Yeah." Duke nods. "You're right. It sucks. But the basketball boys took me in, and I haven't really looked back since."

I look at the photos again.

Duke gestures toward his body. "Sometimes I don't feel like I'm boy enough, though."

"I'm sorry." I turn and reach out, placing my hands on his shoulders. "I didn't realize you felt like that. You know, I've only known you as a boy."

"I know." Duke fidgets, looking down. I squeeze his shoulders. "It feels like I've gotten a fresh start with you. There are no mix-ups, no awkwardness, no weird questions. You accept me as me."

For the second time today, I pull Duke into a hug. There's an uncanny warmth in his voice when he asks, "Is this becoming a thing?"

"I think so."

"Whoa, everything okay?" Jackie says when they come back from the bathroom to find us hugging. We both look over our shoulders at them. "Group hug! *Tabs, hurry up!*"

"I'm hurrying!" we hear Tabitha shout back.

Jackie rushes forward and throws their arms around us. A small laugh escapes me, and I meet Duke's eyes. We share a smile, a secret understanding, and then wrap our arms around them. Jackie says, "Okay, let's hold until Tabs shows up."

"We're really going to do this?" Duke asks, grinning.

"Hurry up, princess!" Jackie shouts over their shoulder. I snort.

"Do we have to have a group hug?" Tabitha asks when she enters the room and sees us.

"Yep," Jackie says, leading us over to her. We shuffle along until Tabitha gives in to her pity, and we surround her with our arms.

"Okay, okay!" she says, laughing. "I'm here, aren't I?"

And it doesn't feel so weird hugging these goons. In fact, it reminds me of the photo of Duke with his teammates on the wall. When we break, I lean on the back of my heels and toss a quick glance back at the photos again. Funny how they don't tell the whole picture.

Duke catches me looking, and he squeezes my shoulder.

"Alright, let's go in the hot tub!" Jackie says, rushing for the bedroom door. We all trail behind them.

"You can't just leave," Jackie announces after a few minutes. We all look at them, expectantly, and they nod toward Tabitha. "Seriously. This is the first time I've felt like I've had real, *true* friends."

Me too, I want to say.

"Yeah." Tabitha lets out a breath and then says, "You know, it's not like I have much of a choice. It's out of my control—I have no say where I end up."

"That sucks," I mutter. I wish I knew what to say to make it all better.

"It's fine. I'd barely settled in, because I felt nervous. I've been with them for about three months now, and still . . . I basically live out of my bag."

We all look at her. I can't even imagine what it'd be like to live out of a single bag. I remember when Mom and I moved into our new house. Mom helped me settle into my new room by putting up shelves for my book collection. A pit grows in my stomach at the thought of not having my mom in my life.

"That sucks!" Duke says.

"Yeah," Tabitha says, scoffing.

"Eden, do you have any ideas?" Duke asks me, nudging me below the water with his foot.

"I . . ." I want to say I have nothing. I don't know how to handle this. I've never been in such a scary position like the one Tabitha is facing.

Unlike her, I've always had a mother who loves me. Sure, things might be tight, and we might struggle a bit here and there, but I've never doubted her love for me once. Not even when I came out. Tabitha having to move from her foster home is so sad. I would hate to live away from my mom.

Then an idea hits me.

"We could write letters to your caseworker on why you should stay in the Middleton school district," I say.

Duke grins. "That's what I'm talking about!"

"You'd really do that for me?" Tabitha asks, looking at each of us. "I mean, we only . . . like, *just* became friends."

"Hey," Jackie says, shaking their head. "It doesn't matter. You belong at Middleton."

Everyone else agrees, and I nod, tugging on my bathing suit under the water. I don't really like the idea of all this being temporary, all this being here and then being gone. I try to memorize this feeling, bottle it up in a jar, and cling to it. *I want us to stay friends.* For a long time. Life, maybe.

When am I ever going to meet people like them again?

When am I ever going to feel this comfortable with anyone else?

Could I lose them like I lost Nikki?

The idea causes a cold shiver to run down my spine, and goose bumps appear across my skin. I try to stop myself from panicking. It doesn't work. I feel the panic rising. My heart pounds hard and fast in my ears, and I can't really see or hear anything. It's all a blur, like I'm on a train going too fast.

My body doesn't feel like my body anymore.

Duke touches my knee under the water, and I jerk back into reality. He mouths, "You okay?"

I bite down on my bottom lip and nod. I squeeze his hand in mine and let go.

21

To Whom It May Concern:

I am writing on behalf of Tabitha Holt. She should stay within the school district and continue to go to Middleton.

This has been her school since first grade, and she has grown into an incredible person. She's made efforts to stay out of trouble, made new friends, and is now part of a study group to improve her grades. We would like her to stay until 8th grade graduation.

Please. Life is hard enough without her mom being around and her dad in prison.

She deserves to stay.

Thank you for your time.

Warmly,

Eden Jones

22

Tabitha is on my mind while I sit in the computer lab working on my English book report. She thanked us for writing those letters to her social worker. I get the feeling no one has really done much for her before. I'm glad we stood up and had her back, because Tabitha deserves to stay at the school she likes.

She doesn't say much about the group home, but she said it isn't the greatest place. There are very strict rules she must follow. What Tabitha needs is a family that's just hers.

I don't tell Duke or Jackie what she said, but I do text Tabitha and let her know if she needs anything, I'm around. She sends back a heart emoji.

The tapping of a pen on the computer monitor interrupts my thoughts, and I look up to find Ramona standing there with her hand on her hip.

"Hi," I say. I'm surprised to see her standing here.

"Hi," Ramona whispers. "Um, did you get my email with my part of the history assignment? I sent it last night."

"I did," I say.

"I just thought . . . after everything that happened with Duke and all, it was probably best I keep my distance." Ramona shifts on her feet.

"Is everything okay?" I find myself asking.

"I just needed to know the exact weekend of your birthday party," Ramona murmurs, sitting down in the seat beside me. "And to see if I'm *actually* invited or if you were being polite."

Nikki comes to mind, and I wonder if Ramona is Duke's Nikki. If that's the case, I don't want her at my birthday. But then a flash of Alexandra talking rudely behind Ramona's back comes to mind and I know. I know that Ramona isn't like Nikki. Something must have happened to make her act that poorly to Duke.

"Eden?" Ramona prompts after a moment.

"Huh? Oh. Sorry." I widen my eyes, trying to focus on her. "It depends."

"Oh. On what?" she asks as she spins around to log into the computer.

"I want to hear your side."

I don't have to specify. Ramona tenses beside me and takes a deep breath. She says, "I don't know, really. Duke didn't tell me at first. I don't know why not. Maybe he didn't think I was someone who could handle it or be trusted with it . . . Maybe I wasn't then."

I glance at her from the corner of my eyes, and she's staring down at her keyboard.

"He came out to his parents first, and then . . . he just came to school and announced he'd be going by Duke and he was a boy. The volleyball girls didn't really react well. And I—I felt caught between them. I didn't know what to do. I didn't really . . . *do* anything. I just followed the volleyball girls' lead."

"You siding with *them* is doing something," I murmur. I feel protective of Duke.

"Yeah, you're right," Ramona agrees. "I can see that *now*. But back then . . . it was new. It was confusing. How could my best friend *not* tell me? Or maybe he did. Maybe I didn't listen. I really don't know, Eden. I was so hurt that he hadn't trusted me that I questioned our friendship—and I picked my other friends over Duke. It was easier, not right. But I want to make it up to him. I . . . I miss him."

And that? I believe it's true.

"Okay."

"Okay, what?"

"You can come to my birthday party—but you *must* apologize to Duke. A genuine apology."

"I can do that. I think." Ramona lets out a breath. "Duke deserves to feel safe."

I smile.

23

Duke and I are walking to the bookstore by ourselves. Jackie had a family thing, and Tabitha has chores before she can go out. And not only that, she has to plan ahead so rides can be organized. Some days, it doesn't work out, because the group home only has one van and seven kids.

But it's nice to have one-on-one time with Duke after everything.

Our phones buzz at the same time, and I pull mine out. I skim the message from Tabitha and then show Duke.

TABITHA: I have good news and bad news. First, they found me a new foster family. There's some paperwork that needs to be sorted first, so I don't know when I'll be living with them.

"I can't believe they found her a new foster family already," I say.

My stomach soars at the thought. Tabitha deserves to be with a family she loves. And then the second text comes in.

"... They're not within the school district, though," Duke says, reading her message from my phone. He lifts his head to look at me. "Crap. That sucks!"

Another message.

This time, I read it out loud. She's anxious and sad to leave the school district. But I've been doing some research into how the foster care system works. Some kids get lucky with their families, but others . . . others don't. And I know Tabitha has been working hard to stay out of trouble.

Duke doesn't say anything immediately, so I don't know what he's thinking, but I feel like I might burst if I don't tell him. "She told me some things about her group home."

"Like what?"

"It's *really* strict. And the staff hardly have any time, with seven kids to care for. So if she has a chance at a real family loving her and taking care of her . . ." I frown.

The air feels heavier between Duke and me.

"What should we say?" he asks.

I look down at the phone in my hands, aware that we've simply stopped walking in the middle of the sidewalk. I make a snap decision. "That we're going to support her choice no matter what. If she leaves the school district to be with the family . . . we'll do our best to keep in touch."

"I like that," Duke murmurs.

I quickly start typing and pause before adding one more thing. I show Duke the message to make sure it's good.

"... 'and no matter what, you'll always be our friend.' Nice touch."

"Thanks," I murmur.

"Think that's true?"

"I hope so." I square my shoulders. "I need it to be so."

We watch as Jackie's message comes in and echoes the same sentiments. Duke sighs. "I really thought it was going to be okay for Tabs."

"Me too."

We fall into a silence when we start walking again, turn the corner, and enter Uncle Moe's Bookstore. I drop off all my stuff at the only free table, eyeing the college student who has taken our usual spot, and sit down.

"You okay?" Duke whispers.

I consider the question before I say, "I think so."

Because I don't come into the bookstore alone anymore. Because I think I've found real, true friends despite all odds. Because I'm finally figuring out where I belong.

24

"Hey," Ramona says, walking up to my locker the next day. She leans against the closed one beside it. "So, volleyball practice is canceled tonight since the coach is sick."

"Okay," I say, unsure why she's telling me this. I continue to grab my homework binder from my backpack and shove it into the top of my locker.

Ramona sighs. "You're going to make me say it, aren't you?"

I glance at her, uncertain how to actually respond to that.

"Yes, Eden, I'd like to hang out with you guys after school tonight . . ."

Oh. *Oh*. Ohhh. She was looking for an invitation and I was just . . . not getting it. I smile at her now, and I'd like to think it's an easy smile like Duke's, but I'm pretty sure it still looks a little forced. I've been working on it in the mirror in my bedroom, though.

"Sure. But Tabitha is still stuck at the group home, Jackie has dinner with their grandmother, and Duke is going to be hitting the basketball court for indoor practice." I close my locker door. "So, it'd just be you and me tonight."

Ramona nods. "Sure, that's fine. What do you want to do?"

"Well, I was planning on going to Uncle Moe's. Want to meet me here and we can walk over together?"

"Sounds good. I'll catch you later, Eden," she says. Just then, I notice Jackie walking toward me. We share a small up-nod before I turn back to Ramona.

"See you."

I watch as she goes to join her volleyball girls. She chats away, rolling her eyes, and it's like I can visibly see her walls go back up.

Jackie puts their hand on my shoulder. "She's an interesting one, isn't she?"

"Sure is. We're hanging out tonight after school." I turn to give Jackie a quick hug. It's odd how normal that's becoming. "How are you today?"

"Pretty good. Got to watch Elijah's face get all red when I made a better point than him in English class," Jackie says, grinning. "I swear, he was about to explode. Just *pop!* right then and there. But he held his cool and made a weak attempt at getting back at me."

"I must have missed that. I've been a little . . . out of it today. Have you seen Duke? He was called out of class earlier, and I haven't seen him since."

"Maybe we'll catch him at lunch?" Jackie suggests.

"Maybe."

I can't help but feel like something's gone wrong. I rub my hands together and hope everything is okay. I don't want Duke to be in trouble. I wouldn't know how to help, and that also spikes my anxiety. I swallow hard and try to take deep breaths.

When that doesn't do the trick, I remember the counting game: five things I see, four things I hear, three things I touch, two things I smell, and one thing I taste.

It takes me a minute to do.

"Coming?" Jackie asks, and I jog to catch up to them.

We go to our next class, and Duke is missing from it too.

I still feel a slight rush of panic before I zip through the cafeteria to find Duke sitting at our usual table in the back. He's sitting alone, looking a little dejected. I slip into my seat and blurt, "Why were you taken out of class this morning?"

"Oh!" Duke says as if he's just realizing I'm there. "I had to hand out some flyers for the updated basketball games since Hurst had to cancel a game. We didn't finish every classroom, though, so we have to do some more next period."

"I'm surprised you're not more excited about missing class. That's your favorite thing." I swallow hard, trying to get rid of the lump that's formed in my throat. Anxiety is really hard to manage sometimes . . . okay, like, all the time.

"They paired me up with Elijah when I could've been with Trey." Duke frowns. "It sucked."

"I get that it's disappointing. How are things with Trey?" I ask, waving to Jackie and Tabitha, who are walking up to the table.

"Pretty sure I'm just one of the guys to him," Duke mutters.

"That must be affirming," Jackie says as they join us. They settle down into their usual seat. "Or . . . not?"

"No, it is. It just . . ." Duke sighs, frustrated. "I don't want to be one of the guys to him. I want to be special, and I want to be—"

"Stop talking," Tabitha hisses, smacking Duke. "Incoming."

We both turn to see Trey walking over to our table. He looks a little nervous and scratches the back of his neck before he reaches us.

"Hey, Duke, um. I was wondering if it'd be cool with you if we partnered up for the next round of flyers. Elijah has a test in French class."

"Ugh, I forgot about our French test," Jackie grumbles. Tabitha smacks them too. "What! Sorry. I'm just not prepared."

"Um, no, that's cool." Duke gives Trey a small smile. "I'll meet you at your locker?"

"Sounds good. See you then. And, um, hi everyone. Sorry for, uh, interrupting." Trey gives us all a smile before he walks back to his table with the rest of the basketball boys.

"Oh my god," I hiss excitedly.

"Holy crap!" Tabitha whispers.

"What?" both Duke and Jackie ask in the same dumbfounded tone.

"It seems like Duke isn't the only one with a crush," I say, looking at Tabitha for confirmation.

"Literally what I was going to say. Dang, Duke. You didn't tell us the boy was wild about you too!"

"I didn't know!" Duke protests. "He's not. He's just—"

"He was stammering over his words because he was so nervous," I point out, eyebrows raised. "Don't you think?"

"I think so," Tabitha says, nodding.

"I could see it," Jackie agrees.

"You guys are just trying to pump me up over nothing," Duke decides, shaking his head. "No way."

"Mmm, maybe not," Tabitha says, leaning in. "Because I spy with my little eye . . . a Trey who can't keep his eyes off you."

"You're just saying that," Duke says, but then he casually leans back, and sure enough, we catch Trey ducking his head as if he hadn't been staring at Duke. "Maybe he was just staring at all of us."

"Trey has no reason to do that," I point out, nudging him. "He knows we're friends. It's not as if Ramona is suddenly joining us or something."

"Speak of the devil," Tabitha says, tipping her head toward Ramona walking over to us. "We're popular today."

"No kidding," Duke whispers. "What do you think she wants?"

"I don't know. We made plans for after school—hey,

Ramona." I give her a bright and friendly smile. "What's up?"

"Hey," Ramona says. She shifts on her feet and asks, "Duke, could I, um, talk to you?"

"Maybe another time?" Duke says. I sigh, wishing he'd talk to her.

"Oh. Um. Okay." She looks at me, a little panicked. "Also, uh, I was just wondering if you guys are going to go to the basketball game next Thursday to cheer Duke. Normally I have a volleyball game then. But it's been rescheduled so we aren't dividing up the crowd." Ramona rolls her eyes. "It's kind of ridiculous how much this school cherishes basketball."

"No kidding," I tease, giving Duke my best attempt at a wink. He mock-pouts before rolling his eyes.

"Do you know how hard it was for me to get on that team?" Duke counters.

"Sorry, I didn't realize."

"Actually it was pretty easy. The coach's niece is trans too." Duke nudges me. "Gotcha."

"You're such a brat." But then I look back at Ramona. "We'll be there, cheering on Duke. Want to join us? Tabitha's trying to get permission to come too."

"I hope you do," Ramona says, smiling at Tabitha. "Maybe we can play more of that questions game?"

"Perception," Tabitha says with a nod. "It's a good game."

Just then, Alexandra walks up to stand behind her. Alexandra starts tapping her toe. I instantly think of how mean she was about Ramona behind her back and wish I had been brave enough to say something.

"C'mon, we have an unofficial volleyball meeting," Alexandra says.

"What?" Ramona turns to look at Alexandra. "Practice has been canceled for the week; why are we meeting?"

"We have to stay on our A game," Alexandra says, and she glances around Ramona to look at our table. "And we don't associate with *these* types of people."

"Oh, uh, I . . ." Ramona flounders. I give her a look of encouragement, and she straightens her shoulders. "*These* people are my friends."

"Whatever." She turns to Ramona and gives her a hard look. "Volleyball meeting. Now."

Ramona gives us a little wave as she walks away.

"I'm sorry that Alexandra treats her friends like garbage," Duke mutters, reaching over to steal my unopened yogurt.

I murmur in agreement and snatch my yogurt back. "Hey! What if I want some?"

"You *never* want some," Duke counters, tapping the bottom of my palm so I throw the yogurt up. He snags it from the air. "Don't worry. I got it."

I smile before looking back to find Ramona in the crowd. She sits awkwardly between two people who chat as if she doesn't exist. I feel bad for her. I nod toward her and Duke looks over his shoulder. When he meets my eyes, he whispers, "Maybe you're right about Ramona . . . but until she owns up to what she did, I'm only being nice to her for you."

"Thanks," I say, reaching across the table to squeeze his hand.

"I don't mean to interrupt this lovely, awkward moment, but . . . If we're done with the Ramona stuff, I actually have some news," Jackie says, straightening their shoulders. They tap their fingers along the table before fidgeting with the zipper of their lunch bag. "I just want to tell you before the bell rings."

We all wait for them to continue.

"I think I'm going to come out to my sister. She probably has an idea already, but . . ." Jackie takes a few quick breaths. "I think I'm going to do it tonight. I've been thinking about it for a while. It'd be nice to have *someone* in my family know."

"We're here for you," Tabitha says, reaching over to put her hand on Jackie's.

They nod, looking down. "It's terrifying. Why does no one tell you that life is going to be endless coming outs?"

"And to think, we're only just beginning," Duke says.

I look at him with a pointed look. He makes a face back because I don't think he meant to be so depressing. Then I turn back to Jackie. "How are you feeling?"

"Nervous," Jackie mutters before looking up at us. "Why can't it be easy? Like it was with you guys. Just: *Hi, I'm Jackie, and I'm gender-queer. My pronouns are they/he.* 'Kay, thanks, bye."

Jackie throws up a peace sign and we laugh, though the tension in the area is thick. I think we're all thinking about different coming outs we've had.

My thoughts drift to my mother. She didn't understand immediately, but she said all the right things: She loves me, she supports me, and she'll always be here for me. I'm one of the lucky ones. Some people get kicked out of their house, or worse. Some people have to live forever in an unaccepting home, knowing that the people they love can't love or see all of them.

I take a deep breath.

So does Tabitha.

"I actually had my first coming out with you guys," Tabitha admits. "I haven't really been friends with anyone long enough to tell them I'm gay. Other than my dad, of course."

"Wow," Duke murmurs. "I'm proud of you."

"You all made it easy," Tabitha says before looking at Jackie. "I hope your sister does the same for you. It's what you deserve."

Tears spring to Jackie's eyes, and they nod. "Thank you. I don't know what I'd do without you all."

Me neither.

25

It's Halloween, so we sit in the cafeteria at lunch in our costumes—I'm a knight, and it's sort of amazing how good my homemade costume looks thanks to Mom. I can't stop smiling today.

Last night with Ramona was lots of fun. We went to Uncle Moe's after school and played some board games together. I made it very clear that she was going to have to go out of her way to really apologize to Duke, and I don't think school is the right place for it.

I invited her to the Halloween party we're going to tonight at the community center—I haven't exactly figured out how I'm going to tell Duke.

"I can't believe Ramona is joining us at the game next Thursday." Jackie shakes their head. "She's such a . . . *volleyball* girl."

I glance over to where Ramona sits with her other friends. She's in a unicorn costume, with glittery pink-and-purple makeup on her face. All the other volleyball girls dressed up as cheerleaders with pom-poms. Somehow, I don't think Ramona knew that was their plan.

"I think there's more to her than that," I say.

"Why?" Jackie asks before shoving most of a cookie into their mouth. I'd laugh if the air didn't feel so intense around us. They've dressed up as Bob the Drag Queen. Earlier, their makeup had smudged a little, but Tabitha fixed it so it still looks good.

"I want to know too," Tabitha says, looking up from peeling her orange. She's dressed as her favorite lesbian from this new TV show I still need to watch—it's a subtle outfit, so most people think she didn't dress up today.

I catch Duke looking curiously at Ramona. He wasn't very original and came dressed as a basketball player.

"What do you see in her?" Duke asks.

I don't know how to answer that question; I see *so* much in Ramona, and I know my other friends don't. "She's not like Alexandra and the other volleyball girls."

Duke considers this. "You're right."

I brighten.

"She's worse."

My shoulders fall. "Duke . . . I know she hurt you, but I don't think she meant to." I glance down at the yogurt in my hands and hand it over to him. "I think you should hear her out."

"Why?" he asks, taking the yogurt from me.

I look across the cafeteria to where she sits with her volleyball friends. "I think she's as lonely as I was."

"I thought you had friends at your old school?" Duke asks.

"Oh!" I scramble and lie again. "I did! Lots. Just . . . just meant when I moved here. Yeah. I was lonely then, and, well, I think she is too."

The three of them turn to look at her, and I'm not sure what they're thinking, but I bet it's a whole new perspective to Ramona.

"Weird," Jackie murmurs. "I wouldn't have ever thought, but . . . She does look like she's lonely."

"I think she was a unicorn to be different," Tabitha says.

"Or . . . She wasn't included in the plans." Duke glances over at me. Quietly he says, "I wouldn't put it past Alexandra to 'forget' to tell her."

"Oh, how sad." Tabitha covers her mouth with her hand.

"Anyway, new topic, please," Duke says, waving his hand in the air.

"I saw this new documentary last night," Jackie says, stuffing some Halloween candy into their mouth.

With the tension between Duke and Ramona still simmering, Tabitha potentially leaving Middleton, and all my lies . . . I feel overwhelmed and exhausted. Halloween is supposed to be fun, and somehow, I've managed to bring my own mood back down. Reality sucks.

I fall silent, letting my friends chat until the lunch bell rings.

26

The community center has gone all out on Halloween decorations. They have a live DJ, some snacks, and fruit punch. It's fun seeing so many people dressed up in different costumes.

"I feel underdressed," Tabitha mutters when we stop near the doors. "No one's going to get my costume . . ."

"It's okay," Jackie reassures her. "I don't think people are going to know I'm Bob. They probably think I'm a random drag queen, you know?"

"I'm going to get some snacks," Duke announces.

"I'll come with you," I offer. This is the perfect time to let him know I've invited Ramona. I'm not even sure she'll show up—the volleyball girls had their own plans.

We walk over, and Duke stands on the opposite side of the table. While I'm trying to get the courage to bring her up, Duke drops the cucumber slice he was holding.

"Duke!" I say, surprised. I pick it up from the tray, and the few ones around it, and put them on his plate. "Be care—"

"Did you invite her?"

I steal a peek at Duke, only to be startled that he's glaring at me. I lift my head and look over my shoulder. Of course, Ramona has walked in, with her unicorn costume on. *She came.* For a split second, I'm overjoyed.

She waves at Duke and me.

"I was going to tell you—" I start.

"Eden, *seriously*? Can't you leave it alone? I mean—she *abandoned* me because I'm trans." Duke's expression hardens. "Don't you *get* that?"

And I do. I get the feeling *so* well. I don't know how to tell Duke about Nikki. How she was my only friend for years and laughed in my face when I told her I was nonbinary.

I can still hear *her* words echoing around me, but I try to push them aside. Sure, her words sucked. But Nikki is the one person I thought I'd have by my side for life; someone who wouldn't abandon me when things were bad. Back then, I couldn't speak to anyone— not even adults—just Mom and Nikki.

She told me she'd be there for me, always, and she wasn't.

What if the same thing happens again? A little voice inside my head whispers. *What if friendship is only ever temporary for me? What if I'm not the kind of person someone sticks around for?*

Tears burn in my eyes at the memory.

"Please don't cry," Duke says, his voice still hard. "I just . . . I don't get why you keep pushing Ramona to hang out with me. She makes me uncomfortable."

"I'm sorry," I whisper. "I just . . . don't you want to *understand*?"

"Understand what?" Duke demands.

"Why." I swallow, hard. "Don't you want to understand *why* she did what she did? Don't you wonder if it was because you were trans or maybe there was something else going on?"

Was there something else going on with Nikki? Is she my Ramona? Did I just not see it? Or were those little negative remarks she used to make about others just who Nikki was?

Nikki made me feel small. Like I wasn't who I am. Like I wasn't allowed to just *be*. And I know, logically, that things with these four are different. They let me just *be*. Nikki had a long list of reasons why she didn't want to be my friend anymore.

I don't think Ramona intended to be cruel. I think she just got stuck in a hard position and made a bad call.

"I had a friend," I start. I fidget with the hem of my shirt. "Back at my old school. And when I came out to her . . . it didn't go well."

Duke's glare softens a little. "Are you saying you know exactly how it feels?"

"Yes. And for a while, I would've done *anything* to be friends with Nikki again." I sniff, glancing over my shoulder. Ramona is talking with Tabitha and Jackie, and they all look over at us, waving. I give them a short smile and turn back to Duke. "At least, I would've done anything to understand why . . ."

"I'm not you," Duke says. "I know why."

"But . . . But what if you don't?"

Duke sighs, and it's heavy. "Look, I'll put up with her for tonight . . . I don't want drama. And if she's as serious about the apology as you say she is, I *might* hear her out. But I don't want any more surprises, okay?"

"Okay," I say quietly. Then I lift my head a little higher and add, "Thank you."

"You're welcome," he replies.

When we join the others, I give Ramona a quick hug and whisper in her ear that tonight isn't the night for the apology. She gives me a grateful smile when I pull away.

"Sorry I'm late," Ramona says. "I was talking outside with the center's manager about bathrooms."

Duke scoffs, but I jump in to ask, "Why?"

"You didn't see it on your way in? There's a petition going around to get Middleton to pay for renovations so the center can set up a gender-neutral bathroom. I said I'd tell as many people about the petition as I can." Ramona shifts on her feet, looking at Duke.

"You did that?" Duke asks. He tilts his head to study her.

Ramona nods. "Sorry. Is it okay that I'm here?"

Jackie and Tabitha glance at each other, but once Duke smiles at Ramona, the tension evaporates for the moment.

Duke keeps his word. He's nice to Ramona for the rest of the evening, even dancing with her in the group dance-off and accepting fruit punch from her with a tight smile. And for once, I don't see the lost look of loneliness on Ramona's face.

Jackie overdoes it on the sugar and gets really hyper; Tabitha comes squealing over when an older kid recognizes who she's dressed up as; Ramona swings her arms around wildly as she dances; Duke pretends to dribble an invisible basketball around us, jumping in the air when he shoots it into the invisible net; and I don't feel so scared of the world when I'm surrounded by my friends.

I want to hold on to this feeling, but I know it's going to be hard to capture when we go back to reality.

27

It's an unseasonably cold day, so we're all cozied up at Uncle Moe's in the back corner. I'm curled up in the window seat with Duke and Tabitha—her legs over mine—and Jackie's pulled up a big, comfy chair with their legs thrown across Duke's.

"I'm glad that you're coming to the game tomorrow," Duke says to Tabitha.

"It looks good if I want to go to a school event," Tabitha admits. "They're happier about letting me out of the group home for that. I'm a bit surprised that I got to come out today too."

"Me too. The group home seems . . . strict," I interject.

Duke gives me a look, but I can't decipher it.

"Yeah. But I've been *really* good at following their rules, so . . . it helps. Besides, it's easier to stay after school because I only need a ride home. It's hard for us to get rides everywhere with only one van."

"Have you found out more about the family?" Jackie asks, their voice quiet.

"Yeah. I learned they're queer!" Tabitha winces as if she didn't want to let it be known that she's excited. "I mean . . . I just—"

"No matter what you decide—if you opt to stay with the group home or go with the foster parents, we'll support you," I say.

It's a promise I want to keep, even if it's hard.

"Yeah?"

"Yeah," Duke says. "Besides, a queer couple? That's really cool. Do they know you're queer too?"

"No, I don't think so." Tabitha bites her bottom lip before adding, "But I met them . . . It's a lesbian and her trans partner. And honestly they're *great*. We had a visitation and it went pretty well."

"You have to do what's best for you," Jackie says. "And it sounds like they might be best."

"Look who showed up," Duke says, nodding.

We all turn to see Ramona strutting down the aisle. Her expression is tight and she's hard to read, so I can't help but wonder if she's as nervous about this hangout as I am. I spent most of last night awake, tossing and turning, trying to figure out how it'd play out. All the scenarios in my head ended in disaster, and I *really* don't want them to come true.

"I'm here," Ramona announces when she gets close enough to hear. She quietly adds, "And I'm queer."

There's a tense moment, and I can sense that no one knows how to react. But I smile and say, "Hi. We're here and queer too."

"The queerest," Jackie jumps in, and I can tell they're trying.

I glance at Duke, just to see his reaction, and he seems a little confused. I would be too if I were him.

Ramona shoves her hands into the pockets of her jacket and gives me a *well now what?* look.

"Come, sit," Tabitha says, stretching her legs out. She points out the empty chair nearby.

"I have something to say first," Ramona responds instead. My eyebrows come together, but then Ramona looks at Duke. "I owe you an apology."

"You don't have to—" Duke starts.

"No. I do. I should've done it a long time ago." Ramona takes a deep breath and then straightens. "And I think your friends should hear this."

"Why?" Duke asks.

"Because most of them aren't cis, and I don't want them thinking I'm not . . . a safe person." Ramona takes a breath. "I've been doing some research—well, a lot of research—and it's important that you understand something."

". . . 'Kay."

I take a deep breath. *Is this happening? Is her apology going to be good enough? Will Duke forgive her? Have I meddled and made a mess of things?*

"I was hurt. You were my best friend, and you didn't tell me you were trans before you told everyone else. I felt like an idiot. Like

How did I not see it? But then, I think back to who I was then. I *wasn't* a safe person for you to come out to. Not really."

Duke looks from Ramona to me, and I shrug. Sure, I wanted her to apologize, but this? This feels like something more. This feels like she wants to build a new bridge between them. This feels like a lonely girl trying to win back her best friend.

"Mona, it's fine—really, I'm—"

"I want to do better, Duke," she interrupts. "I've been trying to figure out how to apologize to you for a long time. When Eden . . ."

"You did this?" Duke asks me.

"Not *this*." I shake my head.

"No. When Eden asked me my side, I came up with some crappy answer. It made me realize that I don't have any excuses for my behavior. I was hurt even though I had no right to be. You were hurting too, and I let you down by not being there for you. I reacted based on *my* hurt instead of realizing you were hurting more."

Ramona bites down on her bottom lip before adding, "I went along with Alexandra and the other volleyball girls because it was easier. It wasn't *right*. It was just . . . easier. And I don't want to do things because they're easier anymore. I want to be friends again, Duke. I want to know who you are now."

He stares at her for a long moment before he huffs and says, "Get over here, you weirdo."

Ramona's eyes fill with hope as she pulls the empty chair to where we're all tangled up together. "Thanks."

I let out a deep breath. I meet Duke's eyes and I mouth, "You good?"

And to my surprise, Duke mouths back, "Thank you."

"So," Tabitha says as if nothing big just happened. "I had an idea that I think Eden is going to *love*. Who's game?"

"I'm game," Jackie says, leaning forward.

I look around at our mismatched group and say, "Count me in, Tabs."

She grins. "I was thinking we could all grab a book we love and . . . exchange them. Like book recommendations."

"A book exchange?" I ask, eyes wide. "Ohmigod, *yes*."

Tabitha laughs. "I saw it in a video."

"Of course," Jackie says.

"Um," Ramona starts. Everyone looks at her before she asks, "What are the, like, rules?"

"No rules, really. We'll pick names out of Duke's baseball hat and then find a book for that person. We'll exchange them and explain why they'd like that book."

"Sounds good to me. I hope Eden gets me. They always have the best book recommendations," Duke says.

I laugh but secretly hope that I get Tabitha. I have the *perfect* book for her but haven't gotten around to recommending it to her yet.

"Do we have to buy the book?" Ramona asks.

"No," Tabitha says. "I plan to get whatever book is given to me from the library."

"Okay, cool. I don't have much cash on me," Ramona says, and Tabitha genuinely smiles at her.

We untangle ourselves from one another before choosing names from a hat. I get Jackie, but I'm still pleased. I haven't recommended them a book before now.

I know exactly what book I want to choose and almost bump into Kevin while I look for it. "Hi, do you know if you have any copies of that nonfiction book for trans kids? The one that dives into the history. I can't remember what it's called."

Kevin beams at me. "It's got blue, pink, and white on the cover, right?"

"Yeah!"

"I know the one you're talking about. We actually moved it to the bestsellers shelf," Kevin says. "It's becoming increasingly popular. But it *does* go into some heavy stuff. Are you sure you want it?"

"Oh, I've already read it. It's right up Jackie's alley." I grin. "I'm so happy to hear that it's selling!"

Kevin leads me to the book and pops it into my hands. "I hope your friend enjoys it."

"Me too." I look up at him. "Thanks, Kevin."

"Anytime, Eden. You know you're my favorite regular." He winks.

I laugh. "You're turning into Uncle Moe more and more every day!"

"Good!" he calls out as I walk back to the corner where we left our stuff.

Ramona is already sitting in her chair, book in hand. She looks at me with an anxious expression. She holds up the book and whispers, "Do you know if Duke's read this one?"

I look down at the cover and grin. "I don't think he has. But he's going to *love* that one."

"You think?" Ramona asks, looking down at it. "I mean, it's about a trans soccer player, which isn't basketball, but I couldn't find one about basketball. I . . . I read it recently."

"You did?" I ask as I climb back into my spot on the window seat. "I'm surprised. It's *very* trans."

"I just . . . I guess I didn't Get It before, and I want to show Duke that I'm trying," Ramona whispers. She runs a finger over the cover. "I was so relieved I picked his name."

I smile.

Soon, Duke, Jackie, and Tabitha settle into their spots on the window seat with me, and everything feels really good until I catch sight of the book in Duke's hands.

My stomach drops.

"Why—why did you pick *that* book?" I blurt.

Duke looks down at the book in his hands and says, "Oh. It's for you. I just figured since it's older, you might not have read it. You're *very* hard to pick a book for since you've read like *everything* under the sun."

He's still talking, but my entire body has frozen in place. I can barely hear him anymore. Instead, I'm lost in my thoughts.

I've been feeling so confident lately, especially because everything feels like it's going to work out—I haven't even noticed how seamlessly things have been coming together. The last time it felt seamless, Nikki Gladstone burst my bubble with her speech.

"You have to read this book!" My own words echo around me. *"I finally figured out why I always felt so different from everyone else!"*

"What do you mean?" Nikki asks me. It's like I can see her as clear as day in front of me: the tilt of her head, the freckles across her nose, her bright red hair pulled back in a ponytail.

I'm shaking. I don't know if it's with excitement or anxiety. But I say, *"I'm nonbinary, like the main character in this book."*

"What are you talking about?"

"I'm not a boy or a girl. I'm just me."

Nikki's laugh echoes around me as if it's bouncing off the walls. She jumps into a long rant about how being nonbinary wasn't a thing. How I was assigned my gender at birth. How all that "queer stuff" was bogus.

But it *isn't*. I'm queer. I'm nonbinary. I'm living, breathing proof that it exists. And I'm not alone. I'm not.

"Eden?"

The voice sounds distant. But then I feel Ramona's warm hand on my wrist, and I startle. Suddenly I'm back in the present with everyone. I swallow.

"S-sorry," I stammer. My voice cracks and I squeeze my eyes shut.

"It's okay," Tabitha says. "Are you okay?"

"Ye . . . yeah." I take a deep breath. "It's just . . ."

I look around at each of their concerned faces.

And I know.

I know it's time.

The story bursts out of me—how that book led to my epiphany about myself, how Nikki scoffed, and I'm shaking as I talk, but I feel Tabitha's fingers between mine, and Jackie nudges me with their foot, and Duke holds my gaze. Ramona's hand doesn't leave my wrist . . . not even when I finish the story.

"Nikki sounds *awful*," Duke says.

"She wasn't always . . ."

"You've got us," Tabitha says, squeezing my hand in hers. "And we're not going anywhere."

Jackie curses and we all look at them. They say, "What? That was a horrible story! I can't believe someone did that to you, Eden. I'm *so* sorry you had to go through that."

There's a chorus of agreement and I let out a deep breath.

"I'm sorry," Ramona says. She glances at Duke and he gives her a tight smile.

"How did your other friends react?" Tabitha asks.

I swallow, feeling drained.

"Take your time," Jackie says.

They always let me take my time when I struggle with the right words, and it makes me want to cry in the best way possible. How kind these people are, how they push me to be a better me, and how they don't push so hard that I'll fall flat on my face. It's their kindness, their patience, and their willingness to let me take my time that has gotten me here to this moment.

I want to tell them the truth. I *do*. But I don't know if I'm brave enough in this moment.

"It's hard to say," I answer. "It felt like once I lost Nikki . . . I lost everyone else."

And maybe that's as close to the truth as I can get right now.

"But I'm glad I have y'all."

Ramona's eyes meet mine, and we don't have to say anything. Two lonely souls understand each other perfectly with one look.

"Thank you for including me in your group," she says, the tiniest tug of a smile on her lips.

"Okay, Duke, you get a redo! Go find Eden a better book, and we'll get this book exchange going!" Tabitha says.

Duke groans. "Can someone help me? Eden's read *everything*."

Ramona stands up. "I'll go with you."

It warms my heart to see them bonding. When they come back, it's with a book I've never read. We quietly clap for this impressive feat.

We laugh, we talk, we tease one another, and Duke even admits his crush on Trey to Ramona. Somehow, I don't think we'll see lonely Ramona too often anymore.

And maybe . . . just maybe . . . I won't be lonely Eden anymore.

28

Ms. Barnes holds her hand up and waits patiently for the class to quiet down.

"Okay, class. I know everyone's buzzing about the game tonight against Hurst, but we're going to try to keep our focus here. Today, we're mixing it up a bit."

I glance at Duke, who tends to sit beside me in class these days. Sometimes we write notes back and forth. But usually we just share looks. Right now, he's on the same wavelength: If this means partners, we're together. I'm grateful because I'd hate to have to choose between my friends, but Tabitha and Jackie are already nodding at each other, and Ramona has a volleyball girl to partner with.

"I have an assignment for you. I want you to write Warm Fuzzies early this year. You have this period and one more tomorrow to write them. I'll approve them and hand them out on Wednesday."

Jackie had mentioned their excitement for Warm Fuzzies, but I hadn't really known what they meant. Duke and Tabitha had said they were looking forward to it too, but Ramona had shrugged it off.

"For those of you who don't know, or don't remember, Warm

Fuzzies are where everyone in the class writes nice things about each other. We stick the notes anonymously in the little boxes I have on the table at the back," Ms. Barnes explains. "Each box has someone's name on it; you'll leave your nice thoughts about each person in their box."

I feel myself starting to panic. I'll receive nice things from Duke, Jackie, Tabitha, and Ramona, but everyone else? Oof.

Maybe the basketball guys will say something nice about me, just because Duke and I have gotten so close, but the volleyball girls? The rest of the class? They've never been around me for longer than a minute or two.

They don't know me.

And really I'm not sure that my friends should be writing nice things about me anyway. Not after I lied about having friends at my old school, and all the little lies that have piled up since.

"Now, if you don't know someone well, I want you to write something nice about them that you've observed," Ms. Barnes continues as if she's reading my thoughts.

Duke nudges me. "Psst."

I look at him.

"It's going to be okay, Edie. They *have* to be nice."

Right.

That was the whole point. That they're nice. Ms. Barnes is still talking about the Warm Fuzzies, but I'm trying to breathe again.

"Five," Duke whispers beside me. I look around the room, surprised that he remembered. I start counting the things I see, working my way down to taste. I move my tongue around my mouth, and I think I can still taste some of my orange juice from breakfast.

"Eden?" Duke says. "You okay?"

I glance at him and give him a weak thumbs-up. He nods, but I can see the concern clouding his face. He puts his hand up.

"What if someone's mean in the notes?"

"No one should say anything mean. The point of Warm Fuzzies is to create *kind* notes. However, if someone does write something mean, there will be an investigation and consequences." Ms. Barnes keeps talking, but I'm looking at Duke with relief. "To avoid this, all notes will be approved by me. But I want to make it clear: The only people seeing these notes will be me and the person you've written to."

He knows me well enough to know I needed automatic reassurance.

Duke gives me a wink, and I slump back in my chair, relieved.

We each get a class list—so no one's missed—and time to work individually on them. I don't know what I want to say to my friends, so I decide to leave them until the end. I write nice things about each classmate, pausing when I get to Trey Danielson.

I write, I don't know you very well, but you seem like a great friend and a great basketball player.

I hope that Duke will approve.

For Alexandra, I frown at my piece of paper. It's not that she's been outwardly mean to me, but I know she's excluded Ramona from stuff before. And that makes it harder for me to find something nice to say.

For her, I write, You're a good friend to Ramona.

Maybe that will make her feel guilty and maybe she *will* become a good friend to Ramona. Maybe.

By the end of class, I've finished most of my Warm Fuzzies. Some are a bit short, some are a bit long, but I still have no idea what I'm going to say to my friends. How can I explain to them—anonymously—that they've changed my life?

29

"Are you ready to go cheer Duke on?" Tabitha asks, swinging an arm around my shoulders. She grins at me, happy to have permission to watch the game, even if she has to go back to the group home right afterward. Still, she's been smiling all day long.

"Yes!" I pump my fist into the air. Tabitha laughs again.

We meet up with Jackie at his locker, and he lets Tabitha wrap an arm around his shoulders too.

Today, he told us he was only feeling he/him pronouns, so I've been doing my best to remember. *I feel like a guy today*, he'd said when we met up with him at the beginning of the day.

"Duke isn't going to know what hit him," he says.

I laugh. While Duke was hanging out with the basketball boys, we spent our lunch period in the art room creating signs to cheer him on. We make our way to the gym, laughing and joking around. Ramona waits for us outside Ms. Barnes's door and she holds up the posters we made.

"Look at them! Beautiful, beautiful, beautiful," Tabitha says, grinning. "Even yours turned out nicely, Ramona."

"Gee, thanks," Ramona says, rolling her eyes, but there's a twinkle of amusement on her face so I know she's not offended.

Jackie bounces from foot to foot, squealing. "This is going to be fun. Duke is gonna slay. You know how he does that little bouncy thing?"

"Just like you're doing now?" I ask. He puts his arms around my waist and swings me around. I laugh hard and playfully smack him. "Set me down! Set me down!"

He does and we both giggle.

"Guys—I mean, friends—c'mon. We don't want to be late!" Ramona says.

Jackie takes off running, and the rest of us follow him down the halls, laughing and chasing one another. Tabitha grabs my hand, and we swing our arms wildly between us.

When we enter the gym, I'm surprised to see how many people are here. I come to a halt.

"Eden, it's okay," Tabitha says, squeezing my hand. "We're right beside you."

"And if you need to leave, we'll step out!" Jackie offers. "Duke will totally understand."

I smile. "Thanks."

Together, we enter the gym and find some seats near the front so we can be right there for Duke. Ramona settles in beside me, Tabitha on my other side and Jackie on the other side of her. Ramona leans in. "Some volleyball girls are here."

"Oh?" I glance over my shoulders and look around. I see Alexandra with her two followers beside her and groan. I look at Ramona. "Are you okay?"

"Yeah. They've just been . . ."

"What's up?" Jackie asks, leaning forward to be part of the conversation.

"Volleyball girls," Tabitha tells him, nodding over her shoulder.

"Oh. Need us to fight them?" Jackie jokes.

"No," Ramona says. She laughs a little, and some of the tension is released from the air around us. "They've been giving me a hard time this week."

"For hanging out with us?" I ask.

"Yeah." She bites down on her bottom lip. "It's fine."

"It doesn't sound fine . . ." I say, glancing over my shoulder at Alexandra again. She's staring back at me, a hard expression on her face. I look away.

"It is. They'll get over it."

"They better," Jackie says, shaking his head. "It's awful, I'm sorry."

Suddenly the game is about to start. The announcer comes on and starts cheering to get the crowd pumped. I lean in to Tabitha, squeezing her hand tightly. It's overwhelmingly loud, and there's a reason I avoided these types of events before now. She squeezes my hand back.

Then the four of us stand up, holding our signs, and start yelling. It's a lot, and I can feel my friends looking at me for confirmation that I'm okay, but I don't look back. I feel sick to my stomach and a little dizzy.

That is, until I see Duke. He runs around the basketball court as if he's some big shot and comes to a stop when he sees us with our signs. He puts a hand over his heart, and then quickly kisses two fingers and points them at us. We start yelling like we're his biggest fans, and I think we might be.

Duke gives us a wink before jogging back over to his teammates and coach.

We sit down.

"How are you doing?" is a question I get asked at least six times during the first period of the game. Eventually, though, they stop asking. Maybe it's because I keep assuring them that I'm fine, or maybe it's because we've all gotten really into this game against Hurst.

"Let's goooooo!" Jackie screams, waving his sign around.

I laugh, feeling like I never want to come down from this high.

30

At halftime, there's a bake sale happening out in the main foyer of the school. Jackie announces he wants something to snack on, so the rest of us follow him out of the gym, leaving our backpacks and coats to save our spots on the bleachers.

We're standing in the line with him while he muses what he might get.

Alexandra walks up to us, her eyes narrowing on Ramona. "You came to the game with *them*?"

Ramona's expression turns panicky. "Alexandra, they're my friends too, and—"

"Come sit with us for the rest of the game," Alexandra demands. "It's only fair since you ditched us for the first half."

"Oh, that's . . ." Ramona glances between us before saying, "Sure, Alexandra. Is that okay with you all?"

"You need their *permission*?" Alexandra asks, rolling her eyes.

"Sure," Jackie says absentmindedly, standing on his tiptoes and trying to see what's on the table ahead of us.

It's now or never, I decide. I have to come clean about

Alexandra. "Ramona . . . There's something you should know."

Alexandra makes a face. "C'mon, Ramona. The girls are waiting."

I catch Tabitha gently tugging on Jackie's sweater to get his attention, like she knows what I'm about to say. Ramona's voice is guarded when she says, "What?"

It takes me a lot of courage. "I overheard Alexandra talking badly about you. She was being really rude and saying how annoying you are. I don't think you should sit with her. She's not your friend."

"Stay out of this," Alexandra says. "You don't know what you're talking about."

"I do!" I protest. "I overheard her talking—"

"You're clearly lying," Alexandra says with a scoff. "Did you write that in that little journal you're always scribbling in?"

Ramona's lips press tight before she says, "Eden, you don't know what you're talking about."

"Exactly," Alexandra says smugly.

"I do! I overheard her—"

"You probably heard wrong," Ramona says, glancing between Alexandra and me. "She's not as bad as you all seem to think she is."

"I didn't," I insist. "Please don't sit with them. She was saying all these really mean things and—"

"Just because I made a big mistake with Duke doesn't mean I can't think for myself, Eden." Ramona's cheeks grow a little red, and she touches her face with a hand.

"Come on," Alexandra says, holding out her arm. Ramona hooks arms with her. I feel helpless as Alexandra looks at me. "It's not a good look . . . trying to tear down our friendship like that. You're going to regret it."

They walk away, and Ramona glances back once, but then ducks her head and follows Alexandra into the gym.

I look helplessly at Tabitha and Jackie. "I . . ."

"It's okay," Tabitha says, wrapping an arm around my shoulders. "Let her go cool down."

"But—"

"We believe you, Eden," Jackie's quick to say. "It's not like you would lie about overhearing Alexandra."

But I've lied about other things. I glance back over my shoulder to the doors Ramona disappeared through. It all happened so fast.

When we sit back in our seats, I notice my backpack is partially unzipped. I bend down and zip it closed. Then I glance over my shoulder to look at Ramona. She's hunched forward, looking at something in Alexandra's lap.

"Don't worry," Jackie reassures me, drawing my attention away. "She'll come around and realize who her real friends are."

"Exactly. Besides, we're here to support Duke, right?"

"Right . . ." I sigh and tug on the neck of my sweater. Gosh, it's hot in here. I close my eyes, take a deep breath, and try my best to focus on the game when it starts back up.

31

When our team wins, the crowd goes wild. I almost forget why I was afraid of crowds to begin with. But then I start to feel claustrophobic as people leave the bleachers. I look at Tabitha, eyes wide, and she immediately knows what's wrong.

She grabs my hand and drags me out into the center of the court. Jackie quickly follows.

"Is this better?" Tabitha asks.

"So much," I say, breathing carefully. "Just . . . give me a minute?"

"Okay," Jackie says, rubbing my back.

I close my eyes, letting my focus shift from the loud noises to my breath. *Inhale, two, three, four . . . hold, two, three, four . . . exhale, two, three, four . . . hold, two, three, four . . .* I repeat it enough times that I almost get lost in it; nothing else matters.

Then I hear Duke's voice. "Ah, you precious, wonderful creatures!"

I open my eyes and see that my friends haven't left my side. They stand by me, talking among themselves while the rest of the crowd filters out of the gym. Duke jogs up to us.

"The signs were such a nice surprise! Thank you. Can I keep them?"

"Sure," Jackie says, holding out the signs to Duke. "But we want them back for your next big game."

"Edie, yo, you okay?" Duke asks, putting his hand on my shoulder.

"Yeah. It was a lot, but I did it!" I say.

"You did it!" Duke shouts, pumping his fist into the air. "It was so cool to see you in the stands, cheering me on." He opens his arms for a hug. "I'm so proud of you."

I rush forward into his embrace and close my eyes. I want to savor this moment as much as I can.

Mom would be proud of me. Well, she *is* proud of me. She told me so when I mentioned that I'd be hanging around after school for the game. But she thinks I've done this a bunch of times before, when really, this is my first time.

A year ago, I would've never seen myself here.

I pull away from Duke.

"You killed it out there. You got more points than anyone!" I say, half shouting in my excitement.

"And did anyone notice how the only person Trey ever passed the ball to was Duke?" Jackie says, grinning.

Tabitha lifts an eyebrow. "I didn't realize that, but now that you say it . . . You're right!"

"We're just teammates," Duke mumbles, but I can tell he's happy about the observation too. "Thanks for coming, everyone. It really means a lot to me. Where's Mona?"

"She, um, wanted to sit with Alexandra for the second half," Tabitha answers.

"Uh-oh," Jackie murmurs, and we all look to see him nod toward where Ramona chases after Alexandra, who is storming at us.

"Alex, wait—stop—" Ramona calls out.

"Eden, is she holding—" Duke starts.

"My journal," I whisper, horrified when I recognize it. "Why? How?"

Did she read it?

"Alexandra, why do you have Eden's journal?" Jackie demands when she reaches us. Ramona jogs up behind her and comes to a stop.

"I don't think that's the question you should be asking," Alexandra says, looking a little too smug.

My heart drops when I see Ramona's expression.

They read it. She read it.

"Ramona?" Alexandra says, motioning for her to step forward. Ramona hesitates.

"Alexandra . . . Can you just give it back?" she demands. "Please? This isn't right. You shouldn't have stolen it."

"Only after their friends hear this," Alexandra says, flipping open to a page mid-journal. "I quote . . . 'I can't believe my mom wants to throw me a birthday party and . . .'"

"Alexandra," Duke says, reaching for the journal. I'm frozen. I remember that entry. I know exactly what she's going to read.

She dodges him and continues, "Just wait. '. . . and I've been lying to her about having all these friends. How can I convince them to be my friends for this party? After losing my only friend at Salem, I don't know how I'm going to do this. But I'm going to do it by any means necessary. I can't let Mom know I've been lying to her all this time.'"

Alexandra hands the journal, open to that entry, to Duke.

"They don't actually want to be friends with any of you. It was all fake," Alexandra says.

Stop. Talking. I want to say. But it's the truth and there's no point in denying it. It's all there in my journal. That Duke is holding.

No, no, no. This cannot be happening. This is my nightmare.

"You have to understand—" I start, but I don't really know what they have to understand. I don't really have a defense.

"So, what? You lied to your mom about having friends and then . . . *made* us your friends?" Jackie asks, staring at me.

"And you didn't actually have friends at your old school?" Tabitha asks.

Duke's reading the entry.

"It's all in there. How Eden felt bad about lying to their mom. How they made up stories about you all—well, except you, Jackie. I guess you were never part of their plan. Everything else is a lie. Go ahead. Read it for yourself," Alexandra says.

"Is *that* why you wanted to be friends with Ramona so badly?" Tabitha asks.

My entire world goes dark for a moment as if everything else falls away.

My eyes meet Duke's in a desperate attempt to apologize, but he's staring at me with a tight jaw. *I trust you*, he told me earlier. He quietly says, "Edie?"

And I can't lie anymore.

So I run.

32

I haven't left my bedroom in three days. I told Mom I was sick on Friday so that I didn't have to go to school. She took one look at me and decided it was probably best I stayed home. Besides, I've been going to school more often than I used to, so this one day off doesn't seem so worrisome for her. She has two double shifts at the diner this weekend, so she's been checking on me via texts.

I don't know what I'm going to do, or how I'm going to tell her that the party is canceled. I can't show my face at school again. I just . . . I can't.

Everyone knows. Everyone knows that I'm the pathetic kid who pretended to make friends for a party because I lied to my mother. Actually worse. *Because I have no friends now.* I can't even imagine what my Warm Fuzzies will look like.

I turn my phone off, even though that's against the rules with my mom being at work. I just can't handle it anymore. I'm staying off my social media pages.

I scrub my hand over my face and heave a heavy sigh.

This has been the worst weekend of my life.

I really thought . . . I can't believe I really thought that somehow this would all work out. I'm so distraught and upset and mortified. My belly has been in knots ever since Alexandra said those words that made my blood run cold. I haven't been sleeping either, just lying in bed, staring at the ceiling, unable to loosen the dullness in my chest.

Really, though, I deserve this. This is exactly what I get for lying to my mother for months. Humiliation.

I keep reliving that moment too, hearing Alexandra's words echo in my head. And seeing Ramona trying to stop Alexandra and failing. And I don't blame her, not really. Not after my poor timing in telling her how awful Alexandra is. I should've been up-front sooner.

About *everything*.

I roll over on my bed, feeling lifeless, clutching my stomach. My bottom lip starts to tremble, and then the uncontrollable tears come.

My chest hurts. The dullness has turned into a sharp pain. I feel weak and uncertain, and dizzy even though I'm lying down. My nose runs and it's so gross having to blow it twice in a row. It's all messy and gross and I feel gross and . . .

Everything is gross. Everything.

I draw my knees up to my chest and cling to them. Sobs are trapped in my throat.

I feel like I'm on display, despite being in my bedroom. Like everyone can see me for what I really am: a liar. I yank my comforter over my whole body, including my head, and take a shaky breath.

My cheeks burn with shame. How could I do this? How could I put anyone in a position to be a fake friend and assume they'd end up being real friends? How could I assume that anyone would want to stay friends with me when they learned the truth? The truth that I never intended to get out. The truth that cost me my friends.

I think of Nikki, the only person I thought understood me better than I understood myself. We were friends despite all my absences at Salem Elementary. She and I got along well, and she never pushed me to be more.

But then she told me that my identity didn't exist.

And just like that, I lost my only friend.

I thought I had found real friendship in Duke, in Jackie, in Tabitha . . . even in Ramona. But I didn't. How could our friendship be real if it started based on lies? This is all my fault.

I should've never lied to Mom.

I should've never agreed to the party.

I should've never befriended them.

With wet eyes, I duck my head farther in the darkness, dropping it to my chest. I squeeze my eyes shut.

Maybe if I just lie here, the rest of the world will disappear, and eventually, this will stop hurting.

Maybe.

33

"What's going on?" Mom asks me on Monday morning. "You don't look sick anymore, kid. In fact, I feel like we've gone back in time to when we were taking SAD days."

She means when I missed school because my Social Anxiety Disorder was so bad.

"Can't I just stay home this week?" I ask, eyes watering again. I lower my voice. "Please, Mom?"

She wraps an arm around my shoulders, tugging me in for a hug, and rests her chin on top of my head. She's the best and I'm so glad she's mine. "What's going on, Eden? Did you have some sort of fight with your friends or—"

"Something like that," I explain. Sort of. Okay, that doesn't explain anything at all. But it's close enough to the truth for once.

"I don't know." She pulls back to cup my cheeks in her hands. "Okay, how about one more day, but then you go back to school tomorrow? You've got to face whatever it is head-on eventually. Besides, you've been doing so great this year. I don't want you to lose that progress."

Except I already have.

And any progress I had was made in the last month. The rest was a lie. All lies.

I'm never going to lie again.

I try not to burst into tears, but I thank Mom and then run to my room. I bury myself in my bed, hiding under the covers, and count my breaths.

Inhale two, three, four . . . hold, two, three, four . . . exhale, two, three, four . . . hold, two, three, four . . . inhale, two, three, four . . .

I repeat it until I fall asleep.

"Mom," I say on Tuesday morning. She offered to drive me to school, so thankfully, I can avoid the bus. I think she figures that I'll go if I don't have to brace myself for that. We're in the kitchen, getting ready to leave. I tug on my hair, unsure how to word this. "I need to cancel my birthday party."

"What? Honey, no. I really want to meet your friends, and—"

"Mom. I don't have any friends." I drop my hands to my sides and bite down on my bottom lip. Tears are almost springing to my eyes again, but I promised myself I wouldn't cry. Not now. Not ever again. I can't meet her eyes, and I feel like I'm crumpling under her scrutiny, but I stand still.

"What do you mean?" Mom asks, and there's caution in her tone.

"I mean," I start, and this is when it all bursts out of me. "I mean, I don't have any friends. I never did. Not after Nikki."

"Nikki was not a good friend to you," Mom says, shaking her head. "But I don't understand. What happened, Eden?"

"I lied. I lied about all of it! It's all lies." I can't stop myself, not even if I try. I rub my eyes. "None of it is true. I mean, it was true, for a little bit, but . . . I just wanted to be better for you."

"Better for me?" Mom echoes.

"Yeah. I didn't want you to have the kid with Social Anxiety Disorder. The kid who has no friends. So I made them up."

Mom sits down at the kitchen table. She motions for me to sit down. "Okay, I don't think we're going in to school or work today. I'm going to call my boss and let her know. And then we're going to talk about *everything*, okay?"

"Okay." I swallow.

After the whole story pours out of me, like it was always right at the surface, I stare down at my hands. Mom doesn't look like she's doing anything but processing my words.

"Honey, I don't understand. Why lie?"

"Because," I say, shrugging. "I thought you wanted a kid who knew how to have friends."

"I just want you as my kid," Mom answers. "I care that you have social anxiety, not because I want you to have friends, but because I don't want you to suffer. I had General Anxiety Disorder growing up, and I take medications to keep it in check."

"I—I didn't know that."

"Maybe I should've told you. I just didn't want you to worry," Mom says, reaching forward to cup my hands in hers. She sighs. "That's my mistake, Eden. But I understand—on some levels—what you're going through. I'm so sorry you thought there was something wrong with you."

I sniff. "It's okay, Mom. I . . . I should've told you that this school wasn't any better. That I wasn't any better."

"I'm sorry that you thought you had to lie," Mom says, collecting me in her arms. She hugs me tightly and kisses the top of my forehead. "I'm so sorry, kid."

"Does this mean I can switch schools?" I ask, hopeful.

"Nope," Mom says, shaking her head. "It means we should talk to your doctor about looking at some medications to help ease your anxieties. And that you're going to go back to school tomorrow. You're going to hold your head high, and you're going to get through this."

"I'm not—I'm not ready."

"I think you are. I've seen a different side of you these last few weeks, and I wondered why. But you've just been blossoming with friends."

"I told you. They were fake friends."

"Were they?" Mom asks, raising an eyebrow. "Because I don't think fake friends take care of you the way they did."

"How do you know they took care of me?"

"Because," Mom says, reaching over to wrap me in another hug. "You told me that Duke introduced you to his family one by one. That you haven't had to do any assignments alone. And you said Duke has never pushed you into a situation you were uncomfortable with. Eden, you just went to a basketball game!"

"Yeah, but I wasn't alone. It's not, like, a big deal."

"It is. We don't go through life alone," Mom tells me. "We're constantly surrounded by people, and if we're lucky enough, we call some of them friends. And those friends we make? They're who help us go through life. We rely on them to be there, and we're there for them when they need us. Friends mess up, and friends work through it. Friends forgive, and they don't just walk away from their friendships."

I press my lips together, looking up at my mom. I think about her words. I think about Duke, Jackie, Tabitha, and even Ramona. I take a deep breath and then I say, "Okay."

"Okay?"

"Okay, it's a pretty big deal that I went to a basketball game. There were so many people! And the crowd was *sooo* loud. I thought I'd have to leave, but it wasn't until the end when everyone was moving around that I started to freak out."

"What happened when you started to freak out?"

"Tabitha and the others took me into the center of the court so I could be away from the crowd."

Mom grins. "That's what real friends do. They look out for each other. Have you looked out for them?"

"I . . . I think so."

We agree that I'll go back to school tomorrow, but we don't agree on canceling the party. I want to cancel it, and Mom wants it to continue as planned. We argue a bit over it until I give up and go to my bedroom.

I check my text messages, but the last one I have is in a group chat from Duke from before the basketball game.

Friends don't just walk away.

I don't want to walk away. I want to fight for them.

34

The next day, school is awkward and horrible. Duke sits with the basketball boys, Ramona with the volleyball girls, Jackie and Tabitha sit on their own, and I'm alone. Isolated in a cafeteria of people I once called friends.

There's nothing worse than being alone after having friends.

We get our Warm Fuzzies boxes and I shove mine into my back-pack without reading the messages.

I barely make it through the day without crying until I'm lying on my bed later that night. My eyes grow hot, but the tears don't come. They just burn at the edges. There's a heavy and dull pain throughout my body.

"Hey, kiddo."

I look up to see my mother and try to calm myself with deeper breaths. It's difficult, and my chest feels so tight. "Hey."

"Was today okay?"

"No."

"Do you want to start up therapy again? I don't have coverage through work, but I make enough tips that we could handle bi-weekly," Mom says, rubbing my arms.

"Maybe," I murmur. I liked therapy. It was helpful. My last thera-pist would be beside herself if she knew I lied about having friends. She was always trying to convince me that I'm likable.

"Did you talk to your friends today?"

"I told you . . . They aren't my friends. They never were." The tears slip down now, burning my cheeks. "It's fine, Mom. Everything's fine."

"Nothing's fine. My favorite person is hurting and there's nothing I can do to help," Mom says, wrapping me into a hug. She kisses my forehead. I want to tell her she's doing everything she can, given the circumstances, but the words don't reach my lips.

I shrug.

She brushes my hair from my face, dries my cheeks, and then cups my face in her hands. "I love you, Eden."

"I love you too," I whisper, and feel my heart break as I say it. How could I have let her down so much? I swallow, hard. I wish I could be someone else. Someone who doesn't have anxiety. Someone who doesn't have to lie to get friends. Someone who is just . . . better at everything.

Mom doesn't hide her own tears.

"Wait, why are you crying?"

"My baby is hurting. Of course that's going to hurt me too." Mom lets out a half laugh before brushing the tears from her eyes. "I don't like seeing you like this, Eden. You were so happy, doing so great."

"Yeah, with people who weren't even really my friends. I befriended them under false pretenses. It's all my fault." I scoff. "It sucks, Mom."

"I know, kiddo. I know." She gets up from the bed. "I'm going to start dinner. I'll make your favorite, okay?"

Mac and cheese with extra cheese. Yum.

"Okay. Thanks."

Mom walks toward the door, and she accidentally kicks my backpack over. Some of my stuff falls out. "Whoops."

"Just leave it," I say. "I'll get it."

"Thanks," she says before tossing a quick air-kiss over her shoulder.

Once I'm alone again, I get up to shove my stuff back into my bag. It's only when I lift the textbook that I see the small box of Warm Fuzzies.

I shouldn't open it. It'll probably be all these mean things. But maybe I hate myself just enough to do it.

I bring the envelope over to my bed and dump the notes onto the comforter. I start picking them up, one by one, and reading them.

Eden—you have really cool shoes.

You have a nice smile and I like your laugh.

You don't care what anyone thinks, and I think that's so cool.

I care what everyone thinks, but you just do your own thing.

I think you're brave.

They all follow the same sort of thing until I get to one that I have to unfold. It's longer than the rest.

Eden,

You're my best friend for a million reasons, but the main one is that you make it so easy to be myself. You don't judge me for anything. You simply accept me as I am. I really like that about you. I see it with our other friends too. You simply take people as they are, and don't demand more or less.

I like your laugh and the way that you stick out your tongue when someone teases you. It makes me laugh. You're so funny.

I reread the message twice more before I fold it up. I set it aside and read some more. I find Tabitha's a minute later. I stare at it for a long time.

You are my first true friend...someone I can trust.

I set it with Duke's. Then I shuffle through to find Jackie's writing.

You're always such a bright spot in my day. I miss you. <3

"Mom!" I shout. "Mom!"

"What?" she shouts back.

"Come here!"

"You come here! I have to watch the stove!"

I scoop up as many of the Warm Fuzzies as I can into the box and carry them with me down to the kitchen. I drop them on the table. "Mom. I think I had friends. Like real friends. And I think I messed it up."

Mom grins. "I don't think you messed anything up. Real friends get through tough times together. I think this might count as one of those times, don't you?"

"Maybe." I look down at the notes. "Look what Duke said about me."

She reads it and her smile grows wider. "Duke sounds like a good one."

"He is. They all are." I flop into the kitchen chair, wincing at how hard I hit it. "What do I do now?"

"I'm not sure," Mom says. "I think that's up to you."

"Mom!"

"I can't give you the answers for everything, Eden." Mom turns back to stir the pasta on the stove top. "But I can tell you this: You've been unfairly ignoring them for a few days now. I think a big apology is in order. And I think you have to hear them out. They're hurt and probably very confused."

I slump back in my chair and sigh.

I'm determined to fix things, but how?

35

"Hey," Uncle Moe says, picking up a book from the counter and waving it at me on Friday, the day before my birthday. I walk toward him, curious. "Tell your friend Duke that his book came in and he needs to pick it up."

"Oh." I fidget with my hands, unsure what to say now. I'm not friends with Duke right now, but I hope to be again. How can I tell that to Uncle Moe? I swallow hard and say quietly, "I'll let him know."

"You and your friends haven't been around this week. Everything okay?"

"Yep," I say, my voice choking with tears. Yesterday and today were so hard to get through at school because everyone seems to have gone their separate ways.

My eyes burn at the edges. I didn't expect to be so emotional about this, but what else can I be? I nod, and then excuse myself, rushing to the very back. Someone's sitting at my usual table, so I go to the spot where we all sat that one time.

I drop my backpack by accident and then give in to the urge to collapse beside it. Settling in by the dusty books no one ever seems to want, I let the tears come.

Soft, quiet sobs overtake me. My legs shake, weak from holding up the world, and I can't breathe. I hate this. I hate everything about it.

I don't know what to say to them, except *I'm sorry*. I'm so sorry. I didn't mean to ruin everything. It just . . . It all became too much.

My sobs slow down, and I start practicing my breathing exercises.

Inhale, two, three, four . . . hold, two, three, four . . . exhale, two, three, four . . .

It's easier when Duke's beside me, whispering the count and holding my hand. I feel tears spring to my eyes again. I can't believe I've made such a mess of everything. I don't know how to apologize. I've never had to before. And it's hard. It's hard to admit that I was wrong.

It takes me a while to recognize that Kevin has come and sat down beside me. I don't know what to do, but I accept the tissue box that Kevin hands me and blow my nose.

"Hey, what's got you down?" he asks when my tears start to slow down.

I dab my eyes dry. "So much."

"Well, it'll be okay." He gives me a classic Kevin smile, slightly lopsided and toothy.

"How could you *possibly* know that?" I ask, surprising myself at the words that slip right out of my mouth. It's weird, talking to Kevin. He's someone that I typically avoid because he's not quite old enough to be considered an adult, but he's not young enough to be considered a peer either. He's in that weird limbo age, and I really don't know how to deal with people like him.

But he keeps on smiling, and somehow, I find reassurance in that.

"Because it has to be."

"What?" I sputter. "That makes no sense."

"Sure it does," Kevin says. "Life goes in waves, you see. There are the ups and downs, and we're just along for the ride."

I blink. My tears are drying up now, and I feel much calmer than a few minutes ago. Mostly because my sadness has turned to confusion and amusement. "You really think so?"

"I know so," he says, nodding. "Sometimes, things get worse before they get better. Sometimes, they get better before they get worse. But it always gets better again."

Huh.

"Always?"

"Yep. Just might not be in the way you expect," Kevin tells me, his tone filled with wisdom. I stare at him. "Sometimes, things happen that we don't like, but it's all for the best in the end anyway. We just have to hang on until it gets better."

"And it always gets better?" I confirm with him.

"Always," he echoes. "Just hang in there, Eden. Whatever you're dealing with, it'll get better. You might have to step up and do something different, but you'll come back into Uncle Moe's shop and thank me."

I laugh now. It seems absurd that I'd come back to thank Kevin for anything other than finding me a book I want. But then again, I didn't expect to find myself crying here beside him either. I look at him and nod. "I hope so."

"Wanna play a game?" Kevin asks.

The idea of playing a game with Kevin right now seems a bit ridiculous, but I have nothing better to do. I shift on the floor. "Yeah, okay. That'd be nice."

"C'mon," Kevin says, getting up. He holds his hand out to help me up. "There's this new game that I want to play."

I follow him to a table closer to the front. He tells me to wait and then he comes back, opening a game.

I laugh a lot. It almost makes up for Kevin seeing me cry, but I still feel a thickness in my throat. I think friends are waiting for us in the strangest places, strangest times, but right now, I'm grateful for Kevin.

36

"You might have to step up and do something different . . ." Kevin said. The words echo in my mind. Now *this* is something different—not for everyone, but for me, for sure.

I don't know if what I'm doing is totally ridiculous or not, but I set up my phone camera behind the light my mom bought me a few years ago. My therapist thought if I recorded videos of myself, I might gain confidence in myself. Mom saved up for the selfie ring light and suggested better lighting might help me with the exercise.

Maybe it worked, maybe it didn't, but now I'm grateful I have it. I adjust it for a few minutes and then hit record.

"Hi! My name is Eden Jones. My pronouns are they/them. I am nonbinary and queer. And I've made a huge mistake." I take a breath, shifting slightly on my stool. "I owe some people . . . *friends* a very big apology. I don't know if they'll see this, but . . . Duke . . . Tabitha . . . Jackie . . . Ramona . . . I messed up. I messed up really big."

I run my hand through my hair.

"I should've never started our friendship on false pretenses. I should have been up-front with you all at the very beginning. I didn't mean to hurt anyone. I was just so socially anxious and awkward and didn't think you'd be my friends if I told you the truth."

I take a deep breath. "But you know the truth now, so all I can do is ask for your forgiveness and . . . understanding, I guess."

I glance over at the door and see my mom hovering. She gives me a big smile and a thumbs-up before slipping out of sight.

"I promise, I will *never* lie to you . . . not again. I'll always tell you the truth. Even if it's not what you want to hear."

"Ramona, I wanted to be your friend because you're smart and funny and a general boss babe. When you walk into a room, people notice. Yet, you seemed lonely. So I thought maybe you'd understand me on a level no one's really gotten before. I thought we were kindred spirits, and I still think we are! Our friendship and connection was—*is*—real. I'm sorry for ever making you doubt that. At the very least, thanks for trying to stop . . . it."

Another deep breath. I brush a piece of my hair from my face and prepare for the next apology.

"Tabitha, I chose you because you were kind to a little girl. She ran off with so much confidence because of whatever you said. I wanted to be friends with someone like that—someone who could inspire others to be confident. I was drawn to you because of that, but you're so much more. You've got such a big heart. I'm sorry for lying to you. I just want you to know I'll be your friend no matter what happens. I'll be here."

I don't think I've ever talked this much in my life, but I also don't think I've felt this passionate about something before.

"Jackie, I hope you know that your friendship has grown to mean so much to me. I would've chosen you for the way you're yourself. You don't let anyone tell you who you are. I'm sorry for the lies I told you, and for making you part of this tangled web I made, but I'm not sorry for you being my friend. No one makes me laugh like you do."

And now for the hardest—or perhaps easiest—apology.

"Duke. Oh, wow. Where do I even begin? I chose you because you're everything I wish I could be. You're strong, and brave, and unapologetically yourself. People light up when they see you. But I need you to know that our friendship wasn't a lie. You made me feel so special, and I'm sorry I made you feel like anything but. I'm sorry I let you down. I'm sorry I hurt you."

One more breath and then I say, "I'm truly sorry for everything. I miss you. Okay, bye," before I end the video.

It takes me a *long* hour of fretting over it, what I said, and making sure everyone is tagged before I upload the video to social media. No going back now.

37

The day of my birthday, I wake up and immediately pull the covers over my head. My stomach rolls at the thought of celebrating with Mom today. She doesn't seem to understand that I *tried* to apologize yesterday and haven't heard anything from them since I posted the video.

I guess I sort of thought they'd text me after they saw it. I guess I didn't post it until later last night, but still . . .

Maybe I shouldn't have run at the basketball game. Maybe I should've stayed, explained myself.

I take a breath.

Maybe. Just maybe I'll be strong enough, determined enough, to track them down on Monday and beg for their forgiveness.

I close my eyes.

I want to bury myself under my covers for the rest of the day, but Mom has a different idea. She knocks on my door. It's *way* too early for this life crisis.

"Go away."

"Coming in."

"Go away," I repeat.

"Happy birthday!" she says cheerfully.

"Ugh."

Mom sits on the edge of my bed and pulls the covers off my head. I groan in protest, grabbing them back, and she tugs harder. "Eden."

"Stop. I don't want to leave my bed today," I huff, yanking on the comforter that she won't give up. "It's my birthday. I should be able to do what I want."

"I know, goose, but come downstairs. I've made your favorite."

That piques my interest. Mildly. "Nutella crepes?"

"With bananas and strawberries and the *good* maple syrup," she says. I roll over to face her now. She shakes me a little. "C'mon, Eden. It's your *thirteenth* birthday. You can't spend it in bed."

"Why not?" I ask. "It *is* my birthday."

Mom sighs. "C'mon. Have some crepes with me and then, maybe, go for a walk. You could go get your free birthday cupcake from Uncle Moe."

"I don't want to."

"Well, it's a good thing that I'm the mom and you're the kid, huh? Up, up, up. Get changed. This is what we're doing for your birthday today."

I go painfully slowly, but I do it. I drag my feet around my bedroom and change into a comfy outfit. Then I drag my butt downstairs and sit down for my birthday breakfast.

I should be spending the day with my friends. I close my eyes at the thought. Friends. Ha. I can't believe I ever thought I could be the type of person to have friends—let alone a single friend. What was I thinking? Who was I kidding?

"So, are you going to see anyone today?" Mom asks, sounding so hopeful.

"Nope."

"Will you *please* go to Uncle Moe's?" Mom asks, sitting down with me. She plops some crepes onto my plate, and I start to scoop out some fruit to put on top. "I'll give you your birthday present now."

I raise an eyebrow. "Is it a gift card for Uncle Moe's?"

"Maaaybe," she says with a laugh.

I perk up then. I can get the book I've been eyeing for the last few weeks. It's about a queer kid who develops a crush on their twin brother's best friend. I can only imagine all the drama that ensues. "Okay. I'll go to Uncle Moe's, then."

She grins, waving her fork around. "I knew you couldn't resist. It'll give me time to get your second gift ready."

"My second gift?" I blink. Mom's never gotten me more than one thing for my birthday before. Usually she saves up for Christmas holidays so I can open more than one thing. "But we don't have money for that."

"Eden. I'm the mom here. It's my job to worry about things like money. It's your job to be a kid." She reaches over and grabs my hand. "And I got a raise a month ago. I didn't tell you because I wanted to surprise you."

"Oh." Then I grin. "That's awesome, Mom!"

"I thought so too." She pushes the maple syrup across the table. "Now, are you excited for your birthday?"

"A little," I say, and I'm not even lying. A gift card to Uncle Moe's *and* a surprise? I smile, a real genuine smile, and say, "Thanks."

"Thanks for being such an easy kid." She sticks her tongue out at me, and I laugh.

After we finish breakfast, she tells me she'll clean up. I just have to go get her purse. I do, and she hands me a card.

"It's not much," she admits, "but it should be enough for at least three books."

"Thank you!" I say, throwing my arms around her. She really is the best. She might not be around as often as I'd like, but she's always got my back. She never lies to me, and she always trusts me. I bury my face into her and hug her as tightly as possible. "I love you, Mom."

"I love you too, my little goose."

38

"Happy birthday!" Uncle Moe and Kevin say in unison when they see me. I give them both a small smile and a wave.

"What's the birthday kid looking for today?" Uncle Moe asks.

"Books and a cupcake," I say. "Mom got me a gift card."

"I know," he says with a wink.

"Oh, right. Duh." I give him a warm smile now. "I'm going to browse a bit, and then I'm coming for my cupcake."

"I'll have it waiting for you."

I pick my first book and browse for my second. My eyes hover on one I recommended to Duke the first time we hung out here. I take a deep breath, but the memory comes back at me so strongly I feel like I've been hit by a brick. I don't know what to do, so I sit down.

It's like I can see the ghosts of us in front of me. Duke running his fingers across the books, him grabbing a favorite series of mine. Me bending down to be on his level.

"Don't look so worried. I like you, Edie. You're pretty cool to hang with," Duke said, his kind words making me tremble.

Then he wrapped his arm around me. "Stick with me, Eden Jones. I've got you."

"I've got you," he said. Tears pool in my eyes, and I stay on the floor much longer than I mean to. I scan the books. There are so many great reads here, and I could slip into a different reality so easily. But this reality . . . this one, I can't escape. It'll always be here. I'm haunted by memories of Duke. Jackie. Tabitha. Ramona.

I was so close to having friends.

No, I *had* friends.

And I wrecked it all by running.

It takes me longer than I would like to admit before I can stand on my shaky legs. I pick two more books because they say *Kevin's favorite!* on the covers. I make my way to the front of the bookstore, smiling when Kevin is behind the counter with my favorite kind of cupcake—peanut butter chocolate.

"Ooh, you're going to like these," Kevin says, pointing at the two of his favorites I had picked. "One has a nonbinary character in it, and I think the representation is done pretty well."

"Oh." I smile. "I didn't even realize."

"I meant to recommend it to you," Kevin admits, "but I forgot."

That checks out. I smile at him. "No worries. Thanks for letting me know. And getting my cupcake."

"I have a little something for you," Uncle Moe says, coming up behind me. He holds out a little bag and I beam at him. "Kevin helped."

"Thanks!" I open the bag and find some really nice notebooks with pens. "Oh, wow."

"We figured that old journal of yours is almost full by now," Uncle Moe says. *Except that Duke still has it.*

"And we thought that since you love reading so much, you might like writing your own books," Kevin says, grinning.

I'm speechless. "Oh! I never thought about it before."

"Well, you definitely should," Uncle Moe says. "But if you want to use them for homework or something, go ahead. We just thought it might be nice for you to have something you could write your ideas down in."

"I love it." And I do.

I hug Uncle Moe for the first time and try not to think about hugging Duke. Then I high-five Kevin.

"It's all perfect," I tell them, clutching the notebooks to my chest. "Thank you."

I remember Kevin's advice and hope I'm on an upswing, that everything is going to work out after all.

39

I'm on a birthday cupcake sugar rush and on my way home when my phone buzzes. I pull it out, curious to see if it's someone wishing me a happy birthday.

The text message I get is from Mom. The surprise isn't ready yet so she asks me to take my time getting home, and I walk slowly. But I can't move at a sloth's pace, so I'm home twenty minutes before she wants me to be.

I unlock the front door and enter. "Mom, sorry, I didn't get your message until I was almost—"

The words die on my lips.

"What is this?" I whisper, looking around. There are *party* decorations everywhere. Mom has hung up rainbow streamers, there are party favor bags beside party hats, and there are chips in bowls on the coffee table. I drop my bags onto the floor.

"Eden! Oh no!" Mom shouts from the kitchen. She comes out wearing an apron covered in flour. "You're home early."

"Mom, I told you. I told you that I didn't want a birthday party," I say, rushing into the kitchen. There's food *everywhere*. She's expecting people to show up. She—she didn't believe me. I spin around. "Mom. How could you do this to me?"

"Eden, honey, you don't understand—"

"I understand perfectly! I *told* you not to throw me a birthday party. I told you that I don't have any friends. This is . . ." I'm at a loss for words.

"Honey, it's okay. It's—"

"It's awful," I whisper. "This is the worst thing you could've done to me."

"Eden, listen—"

"I'm so mad at you."

I watch my mom's face fall and we stare at each other.

And then there's a knock on the door.

"Honey, why don't you get it?"

I feel numb as I walk to the front door. I can't imagine who she invited over to my party. Maybe some family members that I don't know very well. Maybe Uncle Moe and Kevin? I don't know. But I'm not expecting *them* when I swing the door open.

"Duke." The name leaves my lips before I can fully register who I see. He's standing there, grinning widely and holding a gift in his hands. Behind him stand the rest of them: Jackie with a nervous wave, Tabitha with her fuzzy black sweater on, and Ramona with an apologetic smile. "Jackie, Tabs . . . Ramona. What are you doing here?"

"It's your birthday party, silly," Duke says. "Where else would we be?"

"What? I don't—I don't understand."

"Well, let us in from the cold, and we'll explain," Jackie says, motioning for me to back up. I do, and they all step inside.

"Thanks for having us," Duke says to my mom. "I'm sorry we were late. It's my brother's fault. I'm guessing that Eden was still surprised?"

"Yes, but maybe not in the right way," Mom says. "Eden, I want you to know that your friends here came to me earlier this week with the idea of a surprise party. They were supposed to be here when you arrived home."

"I . . ." But I don't know what to say. I have no words right now. I spin around to look at them all, and then I look at my mother. "I'm sorry."

And then I run up the stairs. I can't stay here. I go into my room and shut the door. I'm breathing hard against the door when another knock comes.

"Go away," I say.

"Eden, c'mon, let me in," Duke says.

"I don't want to."

"We thought you'd be happy to see us."

I am happy. Right? It's what I wanted: a birthday party with my friends. I wouldn't have admitted it to anyone, but that's what I truly wanted. My chest hitches.

But I wanted to be able to say sorry in my own way. I didn't want to be ambushed by them. I'm having difficulties responding to Duke, let alone the whole group at my house, in front of my mother.

"Just open the door, Edie," Duke says. "I got your Warm Fuzzy *and* saw your video on Instagram. I know that you miss me too."

I tremble as I open the door. I feel weak in the knees. Duke stands there, and he looks so warm and inviting. He gives me a small smile.

"Come here, Edie," he whispers, holding his arms out.

I run into his embrace and bury my face against his shoulder. "Duke, I messed up big. I should've stayed. I should've explained. I should've—"

"Hey, hey, it's okay." Duke brushes my hair with the palm of his hand. "It's okay, Eden."

"I missed you," I whisper.

"I missed you too," he tells me.

I lean back on my heels. "I'm so—so sorry. I lied because . . . I just didn't want to be *that* kid anymore. I didn't really mean to let it spiral out of control. And really I—"

"Eden, it's your birthday. It's okay," Duke says, shaking his head. "We've all talked about it and it must have been difficult coming to a new school where no one really offered you friendship. And you weren't the mastermind behind the friendships. We all were. We all needed each other. "When I read my Warm Fuzzy, I texted the others to see if they'd gotten theirs."

"So, the video?"

"We'd already forgiven you by then," Duke says.

"And the party?" I ask.

"I called your mom at work right after school." Duke grins. "But we wouldn't have missed this party for anything, Eden. You've gotta trust us on that. We were always going to show."

I let out a little laugh. "Thanks . . . And just so you know, I told my mom the truth."

"You did? Was she mad?"

"Nope." I shake my head, smiling at him. I feel so much better already. Duke's always had that charm, though. "She was surprised and concerned, but she wasn't mad at me. She was proud."

"Good." Duke lets his hand fall down my arm to tangle his fingers with mine. "Want to come celebrate your birthday, birthday kid? You only turn thirteen once."

"Okay."

We walk down the stairs. I enter the living room a little hesitant. Everyone turns to look at me. Duke squeezes my hand for support. "Hey, everyone. Thanks for coming."

"Are we good?" Jackie asks.

"Yeah." I take a deep breath. "I'm sorry. I owe you a *huge* apology and—"

"It's okay!" Tabitha says, rushing forward. Jackie joins her. Suddenly I'm in a big bear hug. I laugh and squeeze back as hard as I can. "Thank you for your Warm Fuzzy."

"And video," Jackie says with a grin.

"I owe you all a thousand apologies and—"

"It's okay. Really," Tabitha says. "We understand. I also have news!"

"Oh?"

"I'm going to move in with the queer couple. Which means I'll be out of the school district for middle school . . . but I'll be going to Middleton High!"

"So you'll only be gone for less than a year?"

"Yeah!"

"Amazing!" I hug her again.

Ramona stands off to the side. After the hugs, I walk over to her and hold out my arms.

"You're not super mad at me?" she asks, shifting on her feet. "Because I swear, I didn't mean to read your journal! And I hate myself for it! I was just hurt at halftime, and Alexandra decided to go through your backpack. She found your journal and thought we could embarrass you with it . . . I tried to stop her. I swear."

"We're good," I promise. "As long as you're okay with me?"

"Yes! And I'm also the new captain of the volleyball team."

"Really? That's *amazing* news!"

"Don't worry—I'm not going to allow any bullying on my team. Besides, as soon as she didn't get captain, Alexandra quit volleyball. I think she's going to try out for cheerleading instead."

"What!"

"I know!" Ramona's smile fades to a nervous expression. "You sure we're okay?"

"I'm sure as long as you don't hate me for lying to begin with—"

Then Ramona practically pounces on me. We lose our balance, and Duke tries to catch us. We fall down on the floor, laughter filling the air, and I feel so good. So whole and complete.

Then there's a knock on the door.

"Who is that?" I ask.

"Better answer the door," Duke says, helping me up. He gives me a quick wink.

"Happy birthday!" an entire basketball team shouts in various levels. Trey stands at the front of the group, holding a container of cookies in his hands.

"Hope it's okay we came," Trey says, grinning.

"Oh, wow! Of course!" I step back to let them in, thanking them as they come inside.

They pile into the living room.

It's a party now. A party for me.

"You don't mind?" Duke asks, coming up to stand beside me.

"No," I say, smiling. "I'm surprised, but . . . honestly, a little touched they'd want to come."

"It was Trey's idea," Duke says, and the soft smile on his lips says everything. "He said since you've been supporting the team, it was the least the team could do for you."

"Eden, come over here!" Jackie shouts, holding up a box. "Let's do presents!"

I glance back at my friends, and for once, a party doesn't sound like a bad idea.

40

All the basketball players hang out for a few hours and leave before seven o'clock, except for Trey. He's been talking to Duke for the last hour, both sitting in the corner of the living room and lost in their own little world. Jackie, Tabitha, and Ramona decide to take some quizzes from a magazine that I was gifted. I could stay, but there's something I need to do first.

I slip away. No one will be surprised to notice I'm gone. They all know that big groups overwhelm me.

I find Mom in the kitchen. She's putting something away in one of the cupboards.

"Mom?"

"Yes, honey?" she says, turning to look at me now. "Everything okay?"

"No." I sit down on a stool at the kitchen island. "I'm really sorry. For what I said before."

"I know, kid. I'd be more upset if I hadn't seen how wonderful you're doing. This is the first time I've really seen you socializing, you know." Mom comes over and grabs both my hands in hers. "You're doing great, sweetie."

"Thanks." I bite down on my bottom lip and then take a breath. "The party was great. I was really surprised."

"Ha. You can say that again." She smiles at me. "I like your friends, Eden. I'm glad we had enough food. Those basketball boys sure can eat."

I laugh.

Kevin said things always get better.

And right now?

Everything's perfect.

EPiLOGUE

I don't think Social Anxiety Disorder ever really goes away. There are always new situations, and new people to meet. But it doesn't stop me like it used to. Not with Duke at my side. Not when I have Jackie, Tabitha, and Ramona to encourage me.

"Let's start our review for our test. Can someone give me an example of what the Hudson Bay Company traded with the Indigenous peoples?" Ms. Barnes asks the class.

I shoot my hand up in the air.

She raises both eyebrows, ignoring other people with their hands up. "Eden."

I glance at Duke, and he gives me a nod of approval. Then I say, "They traded furs, guns, and other weapons. They also brought the Indigenous people diseases and alcohol that they were unequipped to handle as they didn't have any medicines for the diseases or knowledge of alcoholism at the time."

Ms. Barnes gives me a bright smile. "Absolutely correct."

She winks at Jackie, who grins.

Duke holds up a hand for me, and I high-five him. We smile at each other. It's funny how things turn out. I'm not as afraid of people anymore, and although I still struggle, it's becoming easier. Being on anxiety medication has been life-changing.

After school, we go to Uncle Moe's to catch up on some homework and play a new game. Everyone's chatting when we enter the bookstore, and as I pass by the front counter, I catch Kevin's eyes. I give him a little wave, and he waves back.

"Okay!" Tabitha says as we settle into our usual table. She pulls out the instructions. "Let's learn how to play."

It takes us a few minutes to get set up, but soon enough, we're halfway into the game.

A thought hits me and I raise my hand. Duke laughs. "You don't need to raise your hand, Eden."

"I just . . ." I start, and then I pause to collect my thoughts. "I need *you* to know that you're my friends. Like, *really*, truly my friends."

Duke immediately wraps an arm around my shoulders. "You couldn't get rid of me if you tried, Edie."

"Yeah," Ramona says, nodding. "I'm so, so sorry for ever making you think that I wasn't *in* this. Because I am. What I did—it wasn't right. I'm so much happier being friends with you all."

"And I know I chose to leave the school, but I didn't leave *you*," Tabitha says.

Tears fill my eyes.

"We are really, and truly, your friends," Jackie assures me.

"Yeah?" I ask, leaning into Duke.

"Yeah." He meets my eyes. "We're in this with you."

And I believe it.

Kevin was right. It does get better. In fact, it gets so much better that he has to come and ask us to be quieter twice because we end up in stitches laughing. And everything feels good. It feels right.

Because I have friends. Real, true friends. And that's the truth.

THE END

AUTHOR'S NOTE

Dear readers,

Whether you're an Eden, a Duke, a Tabitha, a Jackie, or a Ramona, I thank you for taking time to read this story. I hope you found pieces of yourself—of your friends—within its pages.

This story is for you.

For the Dukes, you are little forces of nature—you're a special kind of person and the world is a much better place with you in it. Never stop being open to letting people grow, but don't hand your heart out to just anybody.

For the Tabithas, thank you for sharing your story in creative ways. No matter the medium, your art will impact the people around you. Don't count yourself out—life *will* get better. It may not be in the way you expect it to, but it'll be the way you need it to.

For the Jackies, who prove that being yourself is the greatest way forward. Being unapologetically you is something unique and sometimes hard, but you're doing your best, and that's all that matters.

For the Ramonas, you make mistakes, you mess up, but you'll

find your way. Never stop trying to be a better person, to be the best version of yourself you can be. You'll get there. I believe in you.

For the Edens, I see you. I hear you. It's not easy being you, but know there are people out there who will accept you for exactly who you are. You're a shining star. Don't let anyone tell you otherwise.

Please move through life with kindness, remembering you cannot know what everyone is feeling or thinking. You don't always know their stories, but sometimes, your differences are what make the best friendships. Stay open. Be caring. Spread kindness.

Thank you for coming on this journey with me.

With love,

Ronnie ♡

QUEER GLOSSARY

This glossary is intended to introduce you to language that queer people and their allies often use, but it is not exhaustive by any means. These are basic definitions, and gender and sexuality can be complex, nuanced, and fluid. We have designed this glossary to give you starting places rather than rules, as people may experience or understand these terms differently than what we've included here. More than anything, it's important to respect people's personal choices, language, and identities.

This glossary was made in 2022 (updated in 2023) with careful consideration, love, and compassion. However, language can also change over time, and if any of these terms become outdated, we will strive to change with them.

GENDER

AGENDER: describes a person who does not have or experience a gender

ASSIGNED FEMALE AT BIRTH (AFAB): refers to someone who has been non-voluntarily given female as their gender when they are born; this may or may not match their gender identity

ASSIGNED GENDER AT BIRTH: the gender someone is given when they are born; this may or may not match their gender identity

ASSIGNED MALE AT BIRTH (AMAB): refers to someone who has been non-voluntarily given male as their gender when they are born; this may or may not match their gender identity

BIGENDER: describes a person who is two or more genders

CHOSEN NAME: the name a trans person decides to use instead of their deadname

CISGENDER: describes a person whose gender matches their assigned gender at birth; sometimes shortened to *cis*

COMING OUT: describes someone who is not cisgender voluntarily sharing their gender identity; can also be used in reference to sexuality (see below)

DEADNAME: the birth name given to a trans person that they have chosen to no longer use; can also be used as a verb (e.g., to deadname someone)

DEMIGENDER: describes a person who tends to be one gender over others but is not cisgender (e.g., demigirl, demiboy, deminonbinary, etc.)

GENDER: a category humans use to navigate the world, used to help humans define ourselves and others as belonging to specific groups such as women, men, nonbinary, etc.; sometimes humans opt out of those categories (i.e., agender)

GENDER BINARY: a system that views people as only being either girls or boys

GENDER EXPRESSION: how someone presents themselves to the world, aligned with traditional or societal gender norms (through, for example, their clothing or hair); one's gender expression may not represent their gender identity

GENDERFLUID: describes a person who experiences different genders; their gender can change from day to day or over time

GENDERQUEER: describes a person whose gender does not conform to the gender binary and/or preconceived ideas of gender; *genderqueer* may be used as either an identity or an umbrella term; some people may use it interchangeably with *nonbinary* and *trans*

IDENTITY: describes who a person is, how they think about themselves, and the other characteristics they use to define themselves

LABEL: a particular word someone uses to describe their identity (e.g., nonbinary, bisexual, queer, etc.)

MISGENDER: when someone uses a pronoun or an adjective that does not reflect the gender of the person they're referring to

NONBINARY: describes a person whose gender falls outside the gender binary; *nonbinary* may be used as either an identity or an umbrella term; some people may use it interchangeably with *genderqueer* and *trans*

PANGENDER: describes a person who is two or more genders and typically feels like two or more genders at the same time

PRONOUNS: how we refer to someone other than by their name (e.g., she/her/hers, he/him/his, they/them/theirs, xe/xem/xyrs, ze/hir/hirs, ey/em/eirs, etc.); different pronouns can be used in combination as well (e.g., she/they, they/he, they/ey, etc.)

QUEER: in reference to gender, describes a person who isn't cisgender; can also be used in reference to sexuality (see below)

QUESTIONING: describes a person in the process of determining their gender; can also be used in reference to sexuality (see below)

TRANSGENDER: describes a person who is a gender other than their assigned gender at birth; *transgender* may be used as either an identity or an umbrella term; sometimes shortened to *trans*; some people may use it interchangeably with *nonbinary* and *genderqueer*

TRANS MAN: a man who was assigned female at birth

TRANS WOMAN: a woman who was assigned male at birth

UMBRELLA TERM: a term that includes other terms or identities (e.g., as an umbrella term, *trans* includes other genders such as nonbinary and bigender; the nonbinary umbrella includes other genders such as agender and demigender)

SEXUALITY & ROMANTIC ATTRACTION

ALLOSEXUAL: describes a person who experiences attraction to other people

ASEXUAL/AROMANTiC: describes a person who rarely or never experiences attraction to other people; *asexual* and *aromantic* may be used as either identities or umbrella terms; may be shorted to *ace* and *aro*

ATTRACTiON: the feeling someone experiences when they are drawn to or interested in another person; different types of attraction include sexual, romantic, physical, and emotional

BiSEXUAL/BiROMANTiC: describes a person who experiences attraction to people of two or more genders

COMiNG OUT: describes someone who is not heterosexual voluntarily sharing their sexuality; can also be used in reference to gender (see above)

DEMiSEXUAL/DEMiROMANTiC: describes a person who must have an emotional bond before experiencing attraction to another person; falls within the asexual umbrella

GAY: often used to describe a person who experiences attraction to people of their same gender, in particular a man who is attracted to other men; some people may use it as an umbrella term for all queer-related identities

HETEROSEXUAL/HETEROROMANTiC: describes a woman who only

experiences attraction to men, or a man who only experiences attraction to women

LESBiAN: generally used to describe a woman who experiences attraction to other women

PANSEXUAL/PANROMANTiC: describes a person who experiences attraction to people of all genders, regardless of gender

QUEER: in reference to sexuality, describes a person who isn't heterosexual; can also be used in reference to gender (see above)

QUESTiONiNG: describes a person in the process of determining their sexual orientation; can also be used in reference to gender (see above)

OTHER RESOURCES ON ANXIETY, PANIC ATTACKS, AND MENTAL HEALTH

ANXiETY CANADA: anxietycanada.com

ANXiETY & DEPRESSiON ASSOCiATiON OF AMERiCA: adaa.org

ANXiETY.ORG: anxiety.org

BRAVE: brave-online.com

COPiNG SKiLLS FOR KiDS: copingskillsforkids.com/calming-anxiety

KiDS HELP PHONE: kidshelpphone.ca

NATiONAL INSTiTUTE OF MENTAL HEALTH: nimh.nih.gov

WORRYWiSEKiDS.ORG: worrywisekids.org

ON BEING QUEER

THE TREVOR PROJECT: thetrevorproject.org

PFLAG: pflag.org

THE SAFE ZONE: thesafezoneproject.com

ON FOSTER CARE

FOSTER PARENTS SOCIETY OF ONTARIO: fosterparentssociety.org

NATIONAL TRAINING AND DEVELOPMENT CURRICULUM: ntdcportal.org

SESAME WORKSHOP: sesameworkshop.org/topics/foster-care

LEGAL CENTER FOR FOSTER CARE AND EDUCATION (LCFCE): www
.fostercareandeducation.org

ACKNOWLEDGMENTS

Thank you to my mother, Sheila Riley, for always giving me space to make mistakes and teaching me responsibility, ownership, and accountability. For encouraging my curiosity and passion. For your unconditional love in the ebbs and flows of life's waves.

Thank you to my fiancée, Juliana Johnson, for being my best friend. For loving me, not despite all my flaws, but *for* my imperfections. For letting me blossom with you and showing me that I deserve love and healing too. For moving through this world with me.

Thank you to my loving grandmother—you are the grandest of them all. To my aunts and uncle for supporting me. To the Johnsons for accepting me into your wonderful, quirky family.

Thank you to Christa Bohan for reading ugly drafts, for listening to my endless podcasts, for always being a text away. I thank the stars every day that you became a "fan" of my writing back in the fandom days. Thank you to the rest of the Boston/NYC crew—Allyson Preble, Sarah Kilduff, and Kyle Hardy—for all the adventures and the ones still to come.

Thank you to Rachael Weeks, Makela Barnes, and Kelly Lang for all those board game nights, endless support, and being such inspiring people. Thank you to Abbey Owens for always showing up, for making me laugh, and those soul-healing hangs. Thank you to Erica Miceli for making me feel seen and heard, for always having my back, and always validating my tough feelings. Thank you to Elijah Abel for always telling me stories; I hope to listen to them until we're old and wrinkly.

Thank you to Jo Allison and Jeff Bennett for being safe, kind, warm friends who always feed Jules and me, and for being such loud cheerleaders in my life. Thank you to Nicole Roberts and Gill Weatherald for being such great friends to Jules, shaping her into the woman I love today, and becoming my friends too. Thank you to Grace Dixon and Dylan Lodge for your gentle love and support. Thank you to Michel Hueston and Ari Conrad Birch for being incredible friends and role models.

Thank you to Lottie Dunnell for being one of my biggest supports no matter where on Earth you end up living. Thank you to Aoife Kearney for being such an inspiration to me and those around you.

Thank you to my Pride5 crew: Jen St. Jude, Kate Fussner, Caroline Huntoon, and Justine Pucella Winans. I couldn't have survived debut year without each of you. Thank you for always listening, talking me down from the edges, and holding space for me. Also, thank you for being incredibly talented so I can brag to everyone that I know you.

Thank you to Eric Smith, for all your wisdom and support, but also for reading some of the earlier drafts of *Asking for a Friend*. You make me a better writer. Thank you to my other writer friends: Rebecca Podos, Ashley Herring Blake, Kelsey Desmond, Ash Van Otterloo, L. D. Lapinski, Jules Machias, A. J. Sass, Cale Dietrich, C. B. Lee, Des Rae Smith, Gabi Burton, Kalie Holdford, Logan Trask, Esme Symes-Smith, and M. A. Kendall.

Thank you to the entire Yellow Gardens: Each and every one of you is special.

Thank you to Eszter Mucsi for being you—because without you, I might never have discovered myself.

Thank you to the librarians, booksellers, teachers, and anyone who champions my books, *Jude Saves the World* and *Asking for a Friend*. I appreciate you so much for all the hard work you do, and the way you hold space for kids who are learning who they are—the Uncle Moes and Kevins of the world. A special thank-you to Emily Elizabeth Fogle, Justin Colussy-Estes, Kaliisha Cole, and Gabriella Crivilare.

And for everyone else who made *Asking for a Friend* possible . . .

Andrea Walker, my first agent, thank you for taking that initial chance on me and supporting me ever since. Jen Azantian, my wonderful and current agent, thank you for believing in me and all your hard work—it does not go unnoticed. Your kindness, authenticity, and determination are admirable.

From the Scholastic Canada team: Erin Haggett, for being the shining star that you are, for the heart you put into everything, and for your thoughtfulness. Amanda Sun, for stepping into Eden's world with me and helping shape it into something even stronger. Gui Filippone, Denise Anderson, Nikole Kritikos, Stella Parthenious Grasso, Diane Kerner, Maral Maclagan, Sabrina Mirza, and the entire team—thanks for making my dreams come true.

From the Scholastic US team: Emily Seife, for all your amazing notes and careful considerations. Janell Harris, Stephanie Yang, Rachel Feld, and the entire team—I couldn't have done any of this without your help.

Thank you to Erica Taylor for providing a sensitivity read for Social Anxiety Disorder, and for the Foster Parents Society of Ontario (FPSO) for providing a sensitivity reader for Tabitha's foster care storyline.

Thank you to Ricardo Bessa for another amazing cover. I am in awe of your talent in bringing my characters to life.

And finally: thank *you*, dear reader. I wish nothing but the best for you in your journey of discovering who you were, who you are, and who you want to be.

ABOUT THE AUTHOR

Ronnie Riley (they/them) is many things: queer, trans, nonbinary, lesbian, neurodivergent, disabled, Canadian. They live with their partner in Toronto, Ontario, and collect books, friends, and cats. They love ice cream any day of the year, birds with long legs, and messy reality TV.

They are the author of *Jude Saves the World* and *Asking for a Friend*, both published by Scholastic Press.

Ronnie can be found on social media at @mxronnieriley, via email at mxronnieriley.books@gmail.com, or online at www.mxronnieriley.com.